AMULET BOOKS
New York

CONTENTS

HOW TO PRONOUNCE THE NAMES

SUEE	SOO-EE	수이
HAEUN	HA-OON	하은
HYUNWOO	HYUHN-WOO	현우
YEJIN	YEH-JIN	예진
SEOYEON	SUH-YOHN	서연
MINSEO	MIN-SUH	민서
BYUNGTAE	BYUHNG-TEH	병태

PROLOGUE

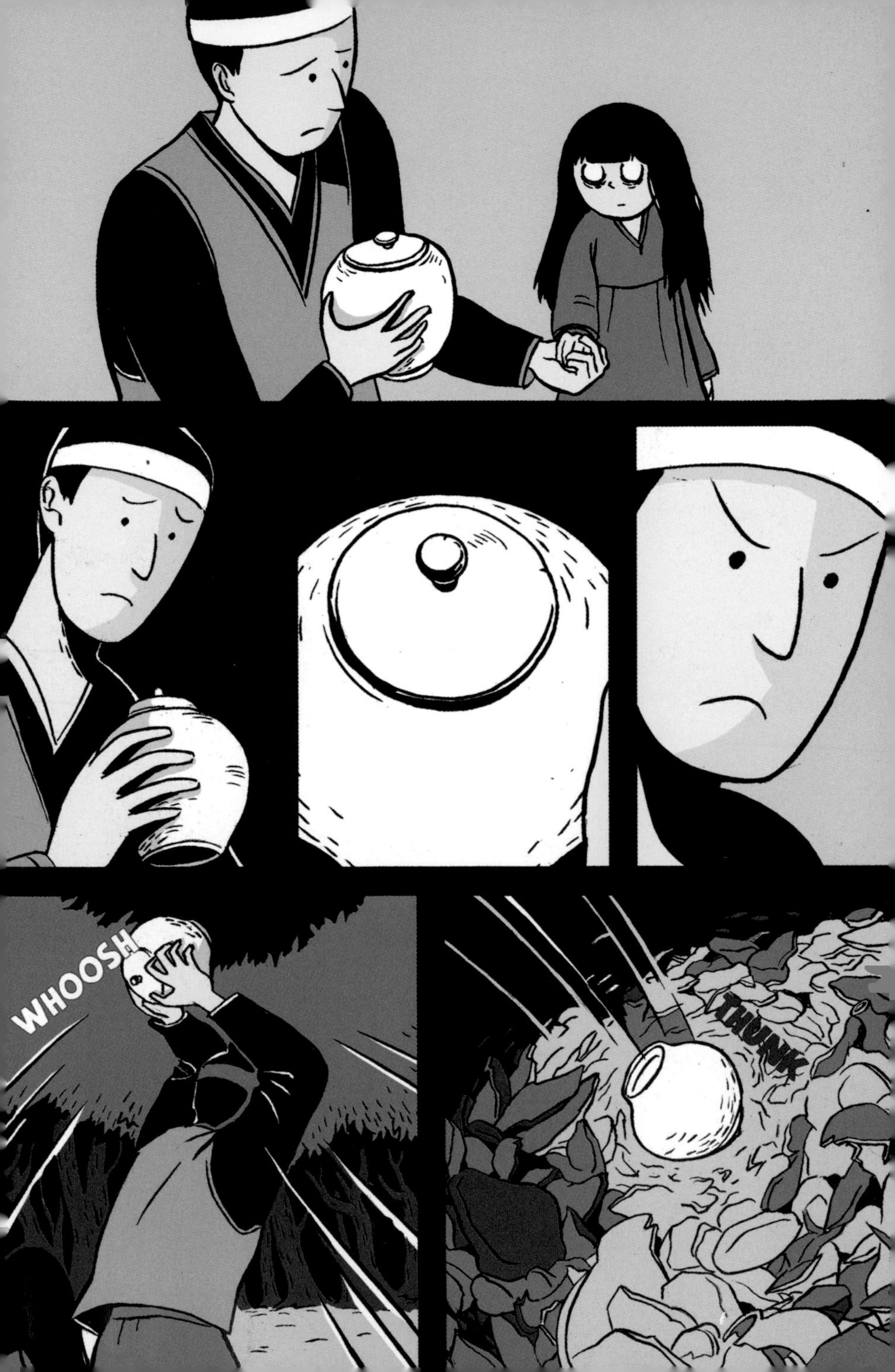
WHOOSH
THUNK

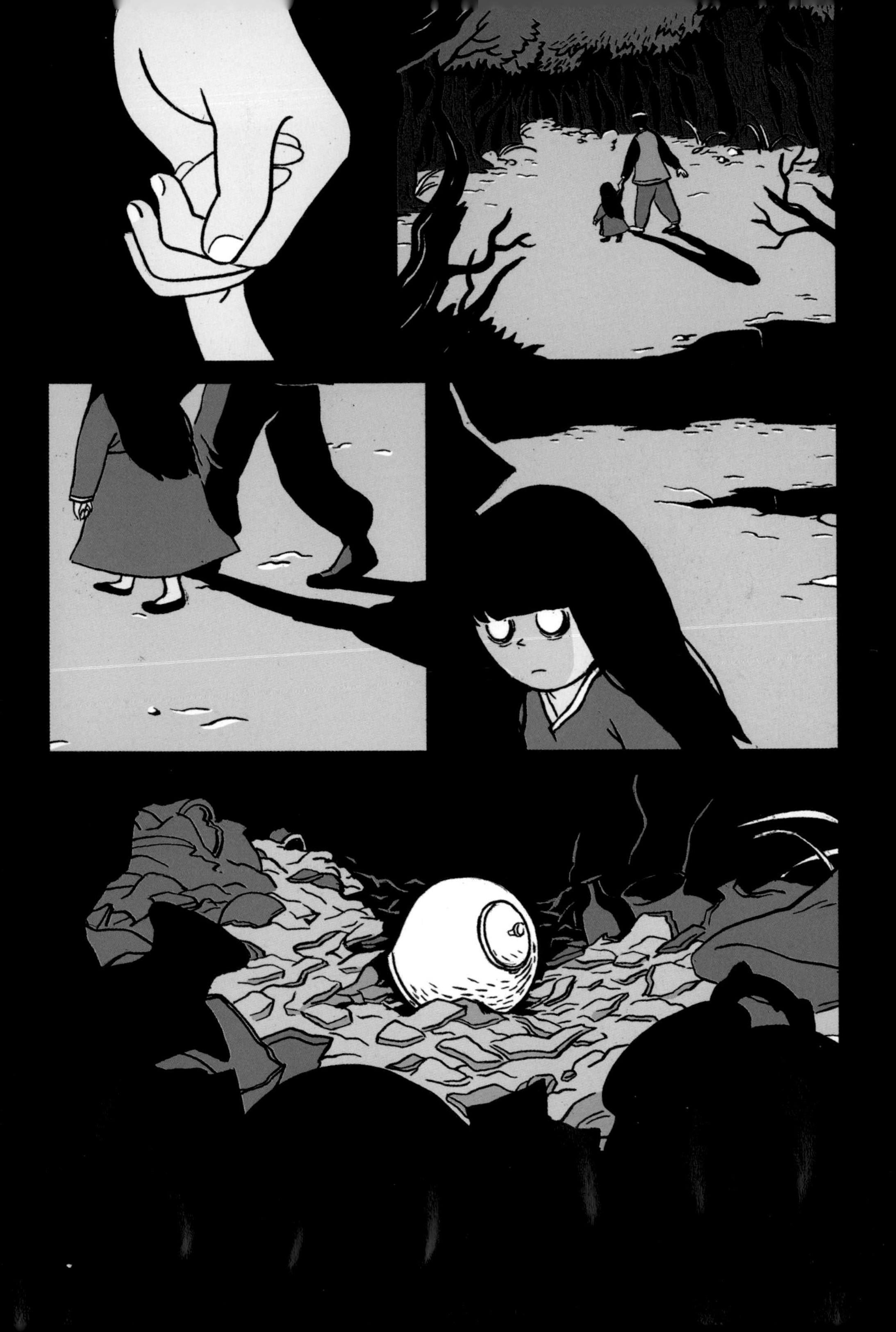

A HUNDRED YEARS LATER.
SEEMS LIKE THERE'S NOTHING IN GOOD ENOUGH CONDITION.
CAN'T SAY IT'S ANY BETTER OVER HERE.
NOTHING HERE, EITHER. JUST A WHOLE LOT OF SHATTERED PIECES. MUST'VE BEEN A DUMP.
I GUESS IT'S ENOUGH FOR TODAY. LET'S WRAP IT UP AND GO HOME, PEOPLE.
YEP.
WHAT?

HOW COULD THIS POT BE...
...IN SUCH A PERFECT CONDITION AFTER ALL THESE YEARS?
WHAT ARE THE ODDS?
CONSTRUCTION SITE: OUTSKIRTSVILLE ELEMENTARY

....
....
HEY, WHY ARE YOU ALONE?
NO FRIENDS, RIGHT?
I CAN BE YOUR FRIEND.
HUH?
YOU... WANT TO BE MY FRIEND?

YEAH. AREN'T YOU LONELY?
SHUFFLE
SHUFFLE
COME HERE...
SHUFFLE
SHUFFLE
IT'LL BE FUN...
TAP

CLEAN...
MUST CLEAN THE POTS...

1.
FIRST DAY
MY NAME IS SUEE LEE.
CLICK
SQUEEEEEAK
I'M A LITTLE SHORTER THAN OTHERS...

SUBJECT \ GRADE	3	4	5
LANGUAGE ARTS	A	A	A
WRITING	A	A	A
MATH	A	A	A
SCIENCE	A	A	A
HISTORY	C-	C-	C-
SPANISH	C-	C-	C-
MUSIC	A	A	A

AND MY ACADEMIC PHILOSOPHY IS SOMEWHAT UNIQUE.

RIGHT NOW I'M GETTING COUNSELING FROM MY NEW HOMEROOM TEACHER.
Shift
Enter
CLICK
STUDENT INFORMATION
NAME
SUEE LEE
ADDRESS
HIGH LIFE APT, APT 101, BUSTLE STREET, BIG CITY
GUARDIAN
MIDDLE MANAGEMENT LEE (FATHER)
"COUNSELING" IS WHERE THEY TRY TO MAKE YOU TALK ABOUT THINGS YOU DON'T WANT TO, JUST BECAUSE YOU'RE YOUNG.
SO...WHY DID YOU COME ALONE TODAY?
MY DAD'S AT WORK.
AND YOUR MOTHER?
AH, YES. THIS QUESTION AGAIN.
I CAN'T BELIEVE THERE'S NO RESPECT FOR PRIVACY.
LIFE IN GRADE SCHOOL IS A SERIES OF TIRESOME EVENTS.

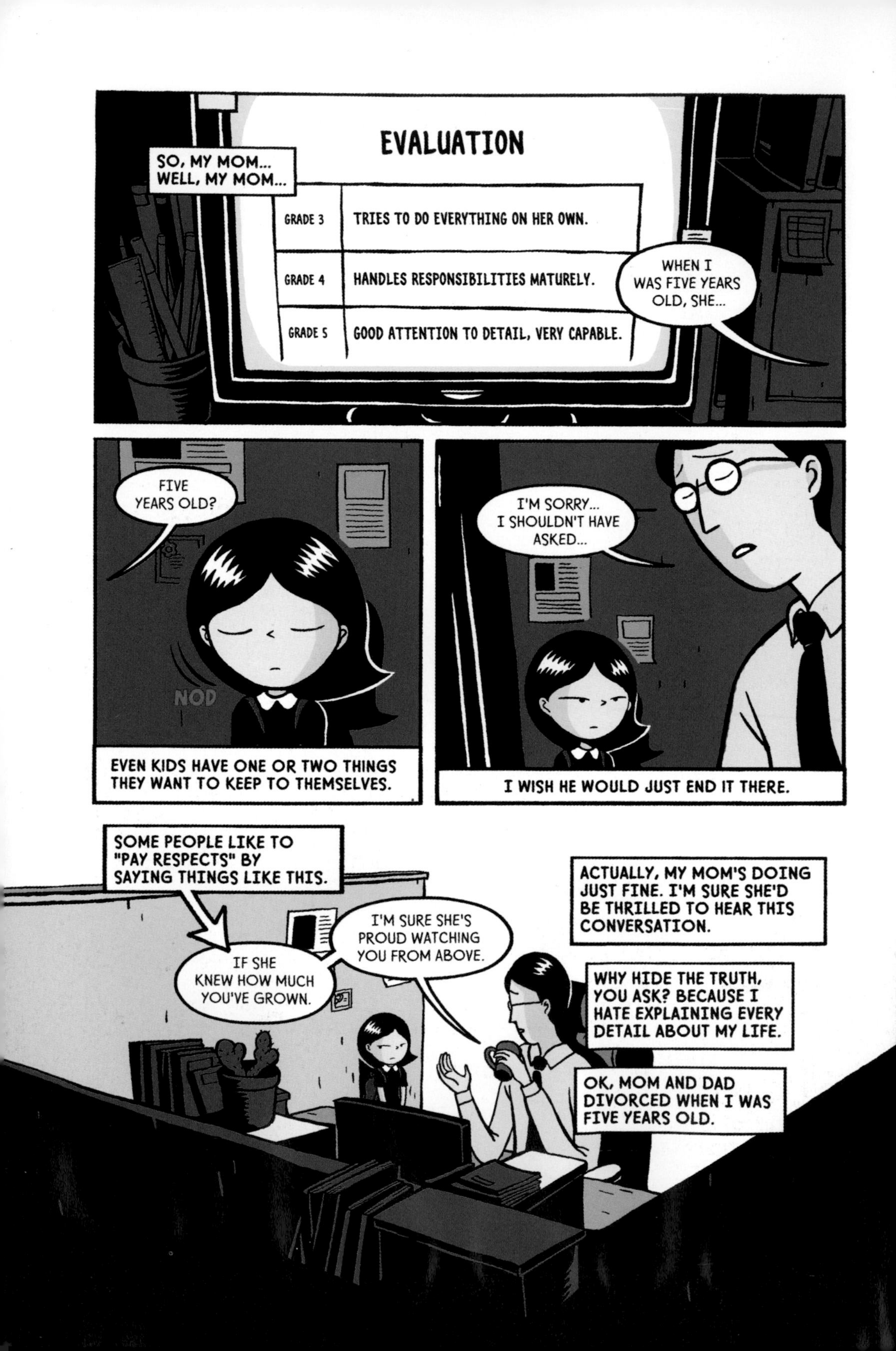
EVALUATION
SO, MY MOM... WELL, MY MOM...
GRADE 3 TRIES TO DO EVERYTHING ON HER OWN.
GRADE 4 HANDLES RESPONSIBILITIES MATURELY.
GRADE 5 GOOD ATTENTION TO DETAIL, VERY CAPABLE.
WHEN I WAS FIVE YEARS OLD, SHE...
FIVE YEARS OLD?
NOD
EVEN KIDS HAVE ONE OR TWO THINGS THEY WANT TO KEEP TO THEMSELVES.
I'M SORRY... I SHOULDN'T HAVE ASKED...
I WISH HE WOULD JUST END IT THERE.
SOME PEOPLE LIKE TO "PAY RESPECTS" BY SAYING THINGS LIKE THIS.
IF SHE KNEW HOW MUCH YOU'VE GROWN.
I'M SURE SHE'S PROUD WATCHING YOU FROM ABOVE.
ACTUALLY, MY MOM'S DOING JUST FINE. I'M SURE SHE'D BE THRILLED TO HEAR THIS CONVERSATION.
WHY HIDE THE TRUTH, YOU ASK? BECAUSE I HATE EXPLAINING EVERY DETAIL ABOUT MY LIFE.
OK, MOM AND DAD DIVORCED WHEN I WAS FIVE YEARS OLD.

SO, HOW DID YOU END UP MOVING HERE?
DAD GOT TRANSFERRED NEARBY. PRETTY SURE HE WAS DEMOTED.
DE... MOTED?
I... SEE...
I READ THE WORD, "DEMOTED," IN A NEWSPAPER ONCE. IT MEANS YOUR SALARY BECOMES PEANUTS, YOUR CO-WORKERS START TO AVOID YOU, YOU BECOME THE OFFICE LOSER. AND THEN...YOU GET FIRED.
DO WE HAVE TO MOVE? CAN'T YOU JUST DRIVE THERE?
I TOLD YOU, IT'S TOO FAR.
HAVE YOU THOUGHT ABOUT WHAT KIND OF EFFECT THIS MOVE WILL HAVE ON MY FUTURE?
UM...
I FEEL BAD FOR DAD... BUT HE REALLY SHOULD HAVE DISCUSSED IT WITH ME FIRST.

MAYBE OVERSEAS?
I HAD TO SAY FAREWELL TO MY BRIGHT FUTURE...
WHERE IS SHE MOVING TO?
I HEARD IT'S TO THE COUNTRYSIDE?
ENGLISH
I'M MOVING TO OUTSKIRTSVILLE.
OUTSKIRTSVILLE?
SO LAME!
HAHAHAHAHA
DID THEY LOSE ALL THEIR MONEY?
AND ACCEPT MY CRUEL FATE.
EXTRACURRICULARS
GRADE 5
STUDENT NEWSPAPER
COMMENTS :
HIGHER VOCABULARY THAN
HER PEERS. SOMEWHAT CYNICAL.
STAY STRONG...
SO THERE YOU HAVE IT. TODAY IS MY FIRST DAY TRANSFERRING FROM BUSTLE ELEMENTARY ON BUSTLE STREET, TO OUTSKIRTS ELEMENTARY IN OUTSKIRTSVILLE.
CLICK

OH, I ALMOST FORGOT ANOTHER RITE OF PASSAGE FOR NEW KIDS.
MAKING FRIENDS.
IT'S A HASSLE BUT YOU HAVE TO DO IT WITH LOTS OF CARE.
FOR EXAMPLE, HERE'S A MULTIPLE CHOICE QUESTION.
QUESTION: WHICH OF THESE IS THE RIGHT TYPE OF FRIEND?
1-JERK
2-LOSER
3-QUEEN BEE
4-DIM BULB
ANSWER: 5-NONE OF THE ABOVE.
HEY, YOU'RE THE NEW KID, RIGHT? SUEE LEE?

YEAH?
OH LOOK, THE POPULAR GIRL IS TRYING TO TALK TO ME. DOES SHE WANT TO BE FRIENDS?
THIS IS MINSEO SONG.
THIS IS SEOYEON HAN.
I'M YEJIN KANG!
I HEARD YOU USED TO LIVE IN AN APARTMENT ON BUSTLE STREET?
MY FAMILY IS GOING TO MOVE THERE SOON.
WHAT FLOOR DID YOU LIVE ON?
I HEARD THE HIGHER FLOORS ARE MORE EXPENSIVE?
THE VIEWS MUST BE GREAT.
BUT THIS ISN'T MULTIPLE CHOICE. IT'S A SHORT ANSWER QUESTION.
QUESTION: WHAT IS THE CORRECT COURSE OF ACTION FOR AN EASY AND COMFORTABLE SCHOOL LIFE?

ANSWER: TO BE FRIENDLY WITH THESE GIRLS, OBVIOUSLY. STILL, THIS IS HOW I RESPOND.
WELL WE...
...LIVED FOUR LEVELS DOWN IN THE BASEMENT.
IT WAS DARK LIKE A DUNGEON.
OH, AND I WOULD SEE SNAKES...
WHAT?
YOU LIVED IN THE BASEMENT LEVEL?
WHAT DID YOU SAY?
DID SHE SAY SNAKES?
I CAN TELL WITH A FEW JOKES IF THESE GIRLS ARE ON MY LEVEL OR NOT.
CLEARLY THESE GIRLS AREN'T. THEY'RE WAY TOO SERIOUS, CAN'T SEE A JOKE THAT'S RIGHT IN FRONT OF THEM.
THEREFORE, PASS.
SEE YOU...
WHAT A FREAK!

I AM JUST A SEMESTER AWAY FROM FINISHING ELEMENTARY SCHOOL.
I JUST NEED TO GET THROUGH THREE MONTHS, AND THEN IT'S BYE-BYE TO THIS PLACE. LAST DAY OF SCHOOL, PLEASE GET HERE ASAP!
HEY...
HEY...
...COME HERE!
WHAT?!
EXHIBIT ROOM
CREEEAAAAK

WHO CALLED ME?
I DID...
AND YOU ARE?
THE EXHIBIT ROOM IS LIKE A WAREHOUSE...
AND THERE ARE SO MANY POTS HERE...
I'LL BE YOUR FRIEND...

MY...FRIEND?
SORRY, BUT NO THANKS.
WHY?
YOU DON'T HAVE ANY FRIENDS...
I JUST TRANSFERRED HERE, OK? IT'S NORMAL NOT TO HAVE FRIENDS YET.
ANYWAY, HOW DOES SHE EXPECT TO BE FRIENDS IF SHE'S HIDING FROM ME? HOW WEIRD.
WAIT...HOLD ON!
I DON'T...
...HAVE A MOM EITHER!

WHAT?
STEP
STEP
H-HOW... DID YOU KNOW THAT?
I KNOW EVERYTHING...

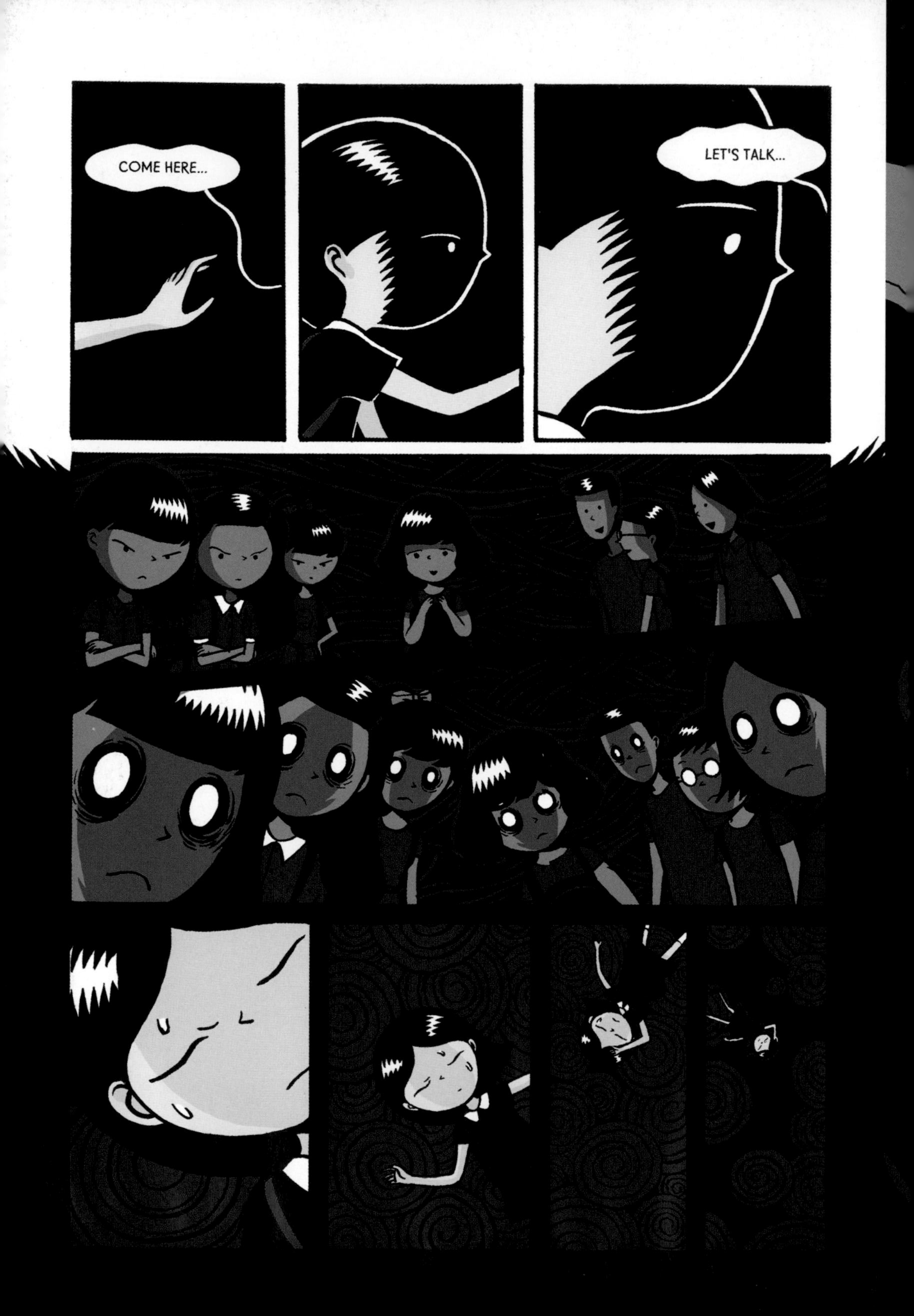
COME HERE...
LET'S TALK...

IT'LL BE FUN...
MUH...NNNG...

MOM!!!
PANT
PANT
PANT
ROCK
SUEE'S ROOM
WAS IT... A DREAM?

2.
UNINVITED
DAD, WHAT'S WITH THE HOUSE?
IT'S BUILT RIGHT BETWEEN TWO BUILDINGS? IS IT EVEN LEGAL?
THAT'S WHY IT'S CALLED "BETWEEN HOUSE." EACH HOUSE IN THIS NEIGHBORHOOD HAS A NAME. WHATCHA THINK?
SERIOUSLY? NOT "ADORABLE COTTAGE" OR "LITTLE TOWER" OR EVEN "QUAINT APARTMENT," BUT "BETWEEN HOUSE?"
IT'S CLOSE TO MY OFFICE SO I'LL BE HOME EARLIER. I'LL MAKE YOU SOMETHING YUMMY FOR DINNER EVERY DAY.
HAIR S
OPEN

ARE YOU SURE THAT THERE'S EVEN ENOUGH ROOM IN THIS HOUSE FOR A KITCHEN?
THAT'S VERY FUNNY.
IN MY DREAMS...
DAD IS A MASTER CHEF.
HE CAN MAKE ANY DISH, AND IT'S SO GOOD THAT NO ONE CAN RESIST HIS COOKING.
BUT IN REALITY...

...HE NEVER COOKS. IN FACT, HE USES THE KITCHEN AS EXTRA STORAGE!
OFF TO WORK EARLY. HAVE A GREAT DAY AT SCHOOL.

DREAMS ARE JUST DREAMS.
CRINKLE

THEY SAY KIDS GROW ON DREAMS, RIGHT?
BEER
MILK
JAM
BISCUIT
WHICH IS WHY NIGHTMARES ARE BAD FOR DEVELOPMENT?
BUT THEY ARE WRONG. GROWING CHILDREN...
...GROW ON MILK!
AW, SO ANNOYING! TOO BUSY WITH THE MOVE, IS THAT IT?
CLOP

OH, COME ON! SHOULDN'T A FATHER AT LEAST KNOW TO LEAVE ENOUGH MILK FOR HIS DAUGHTER?
YOUR ONLY DAUGHTER IS ALSO BUSY ADJUSTING TO A NEW SCHOOL, YOU KNOW?
MILK
MILK
YOU COULD USE THE DIET.
I'M A GROWING CHILD, OK? I NEED MY NUTRIENTS FOR DEVELOPMENT. NO WAY I NEED TO DIET.
BESIDES, I'M TOO SKINNY ANYWAY.
THEN HURRY UP AND DRINK IT.
WHAT DO YOU CARE IF I DRINK IT OR NOT...
WAIT A MINUTE...
WHO...AM I TALKING TO?

OVER HERE...
WHERE?
LOOK...AT YOUR FEET!
TURN
SOMETHING IS...
MILK
MILK
BISCUIT
WATCHING ME?!
IS IT...MY SHADOW?
NO, THAT'S...

...UNMISTAKABLY...
...A GHOST! YOU'RE A GHOST!
COME ON, I'M NOT A GHOST!
NOT A GHOST? THEN...
LOOK CAREFULLY!
...THIS IS ALL A DREAM!
I NEED TO GET OUT OF HERE. HOW DO I WAKE UP?
WHERE ARE YOU GOING?
WAKE UP, WAKE UP!
SHE'S FREAKING ME OUT!
I'LL RUN AWAY FIRST...
MAYBE SHE'LL DISAPPEAR!

FOCUS... FOCUS...
YOU KNOW...
I'M NOT GOING AWAY! LOOK HERE!
YOU STILL CAN'T TELL?
SHE'S STILL HERE!
SUEE LEE! WAKE UP! NOW!
DON'T THINK TOO HARD. LOOK!
AT YOUR FEET!
MY FEET?
YEAH, THERE. DO YOU SEE NOW?

OK, SHE'S STUCK TO MY FEET...SO LET'S SAY SHE REALLY IS MY SHADOW.
BUT...
SHADOWS DON'T MOVE OR SPEAK. SECOND, IF YOU'RE MY SHADOW, YOU EXIST BECAUSE LIGHT CAN'T GET THROUGH MY BODY, SO YOU SHOULD MOVE THE SAME AS ME. BUT YOU'RE ALL OVER THE PLACE.
THEREFORE, THIS IS ALL A DREAM. A NIGHTMARE. AND YOU ARE NOT MY SHADOW!
SAY WHATEVER YOU WANT, BUT I STILL CAN'T SEPARATE FROM YOUR FEET.
IT'S TRUE...
THIS NIGHTMARE FEELS VERY REAL. SO...IS SHE REAL?
NO. I WON'T TAKE HER WORD FOR IT. I NEED TO FIGURE THIS OUT!
HEY, WHAT IS IT THIS TIME?
I DON'T KNOW WHAT YOU'RE THINKING, BUT...

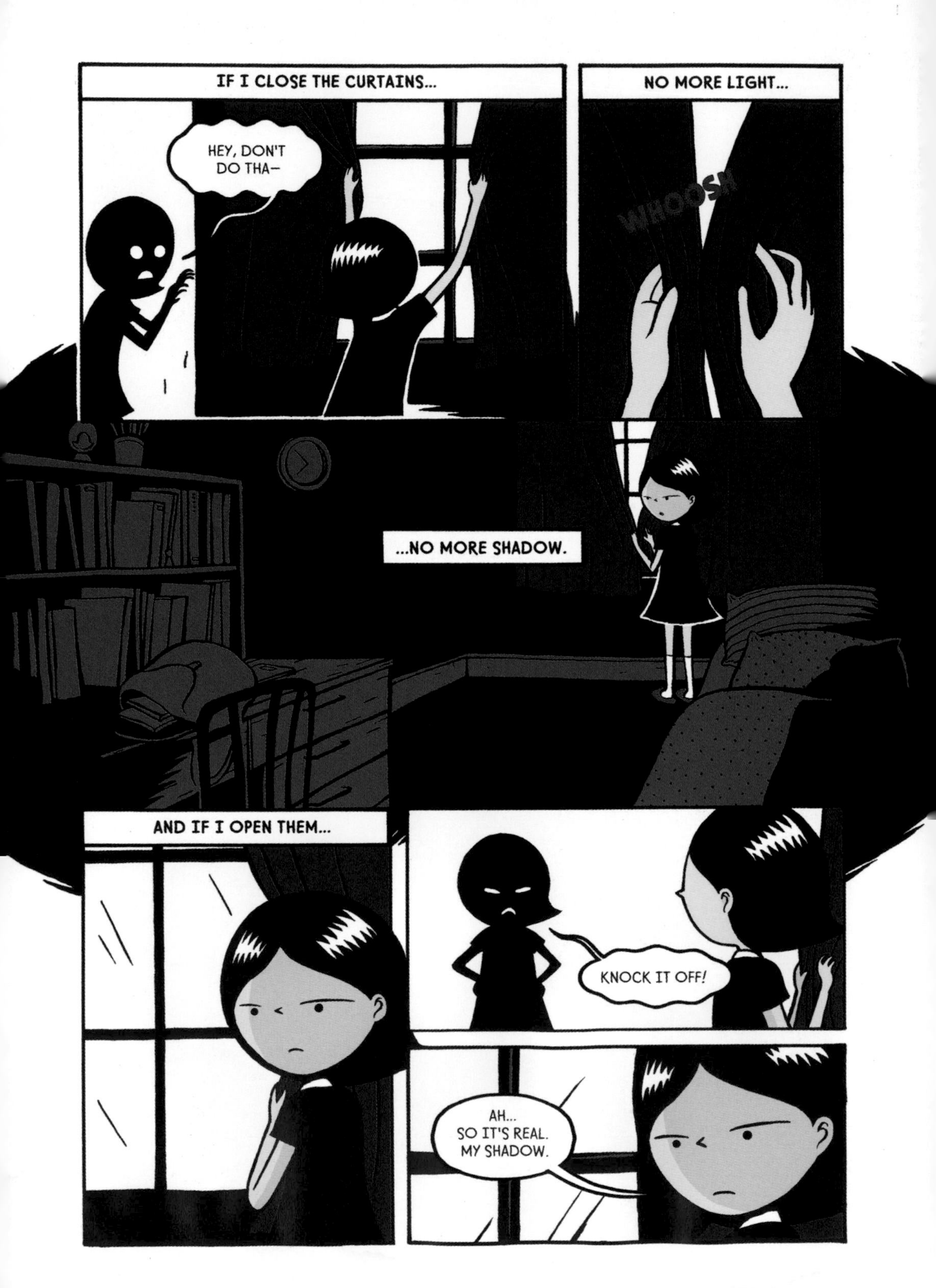
IF I CLOSE THE CURTAINS...
HEY, DON'T DO THA—
NO MORE LIGHT...
WHOOSH
...NO MORE SHADOW.
AND IF I OPEN THEM...
KNOCK IT OFF!
AH... SO IT'S REAL. MY SHADOW.

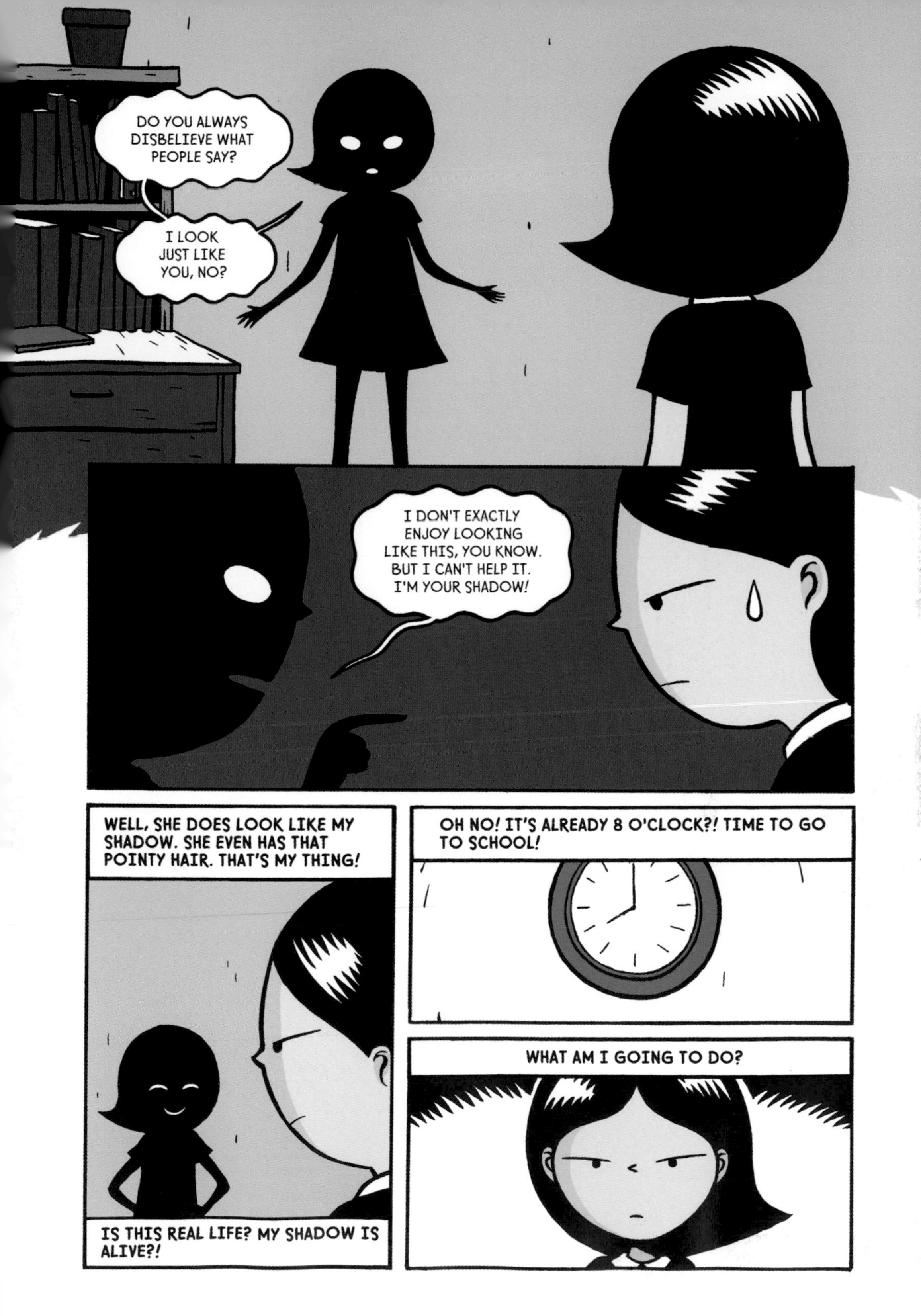
DO YOU ALWAYS DISBELIEVE WHAT PEOPLE SAY?
I LOOK JUST LIKE YOU, NO?
I DON'T EXACTLY ENJOY LOOKING LIKE THIS, YOU KNOW. BUT I CAN'T HELP IT. I'M YOUR SHADOW!
WELL, SHE DOES LOOK LIKE MY SHADOW. SHE EVEN HAS THAT POINTY HAIR. THAT'S MY THING!
IS THIS REAL LIFE? MY SHADOW IS ALIVE?!
OH NO! IT'S ALREADY 8 O'CLOCK?! TIME TO GO TO SCHOOL!
WHAT AM I GOING TO DO?

DO I GO TO SCHOOL LIKE THIS? WITH A TALKING SHADOW AT MY HEELS? OR SHOULD I STAY HOME?
BUT IF I SKIP SCHOOL...I CAN'T GET THE PERFECT ATTENDANCE AWARD!
TAKE ME TO SCHOOL. I'LL BE QUIET
WHY SHOULD I BELIEVE YOU?
BECAUSE YOU HAVE NO CHOICE.
WH-WHAT?
TRY ASKING NICELY!
IF I ASK, WILL YOU LISTEN?
DEPENDS HOW YOU ASK.
NO, WE'LL DO THIS MY WAY. IF YOU CAUSE ME ANY TROUBLE AT SCHOOL, I'M GOING TO GO INTO THE SHADE.
IS THAT A THREAT?
FINE. SINCE IT'S THE FIRST TIME, I'LL BE DEAD QUIET.
ARE YOU NEGOTIATING WITH ME?
WHY? YOU DON'T WANT ME TO BE QUIET?
WH-WHEN DID I SAY THAT?
GOOD, THEN TRUST ME! I PROMISE I'LL BE TOTALLY QUIET.
PLEASE, PLEASE, PLEASE! PLEASE LET NOTHING HAPPEN...

What's the matter?
무슨 일 있니?
I have (a fever).
나 열이 나.
You should (go to
의사에게 가봐야겠다.
OK. LISTEN CAREFULLY. LET'S TRY ONE MORE TIME.
WHAT'S THE MATTER?
TEACHER... MUST CLEAN.
I SAID, REPEAT WHAT IT SAYS ON THE BLACKBOARD...
HAHAHAHAHAHA
WHY IS EVERYONE LAUGHING?
SHH! BE QUIET!
SWISH
HEY! SUEE! WHAT DID YOU JUST SAY?
MIND YOUR OWN BUSINESS!

...ONCE SOMEONE LEARNS A FALSE IDEA...
BLAH BLAH... BLAH BLAH...
HELP...WHEN...IS IT...OVER? I CAN'T...STAY HERE...ANY... LONGER...
LOOKS LIKE THE SHADOW WENT AWAY. MAYBE IT'S BECAUSE THE ROOM IS DARK. GOOD RIDDANCE. LOOKS LIKE NO ONE NOTICED, EITHER.
...CHANGE IN ORBITS ACCORDING TO GRAVITY...
BLAH BLAH... BLAH BLAH...
STILL...WHAT A LONG DAY.
AND YEJIN KANG...
IF SHE FINDS OUT ABOUT MY SHADOW, I'LL NEVER HEAR THE END OF IT.

TIME FOR P.E., SO CHANGE INTO YOUR GYM CLOTHES AND MEET ME ON THE FIELD.
THE FIELD?
WE'RE GOING OUTSIDE, AND THE SUN IS SO STRONG. EVERYONE'S GOING TO SEE MY SHADOW!
SHINE
I NEVER LIE OR BEND RULES.
IF I DON'T WANT TO DO SOMETHING I'M HONEST ABOUT WHAT MY REASONS ARE.
BUT IN THIS CASE...
YOU'RE FEELING... SICK?
THIS IS NOT A SITUATION I CAN EXPLAIN THROUGH LOGIC. I'LL HAVE TO LIE.
OF COURSE, IT'S A LIE WITH GOOD CAUSE.
AS LONG AS I'M LYING, I NEED TO PICK A LIE THAT PEOPLE WILL BELIEVE. SOMETHING THAT...TRIGGERS PITY.
YES... MY HEAD IS... SUDDENLY POUNDING.
I THINK IT'S LACK OF NUTRITION. OR MAYBE I HAVEN'T BEEN GETTING ENOUGH SLEEP.
OH DEAR...

CREEEAK
HE NURSE IS IN
NOT ENOUGH THIS WAY...
NOT ENOUGH THAT WAY...WHAT A MYSTERY...
WHY DON'T YOU SIT DOWN THERE AND WAIT A SECOND?
I'LL TAKE A LOOK ONCE I FINISH THIS.
SOMEONE'S HERE? DITCHING CLASS?
LET'S SEE...

WHAT'S THE MATTER TODAY?
I HAVE A BAD HEADACHE AND NEED TO REST.
DID YOU TAKE THE MEDICINE I GAVE YOU YESTERDAY BEFORE SLEEPING?
MEDICINE?
TSK TSK TSK
I TOLD YOU TO TAKE IT BEFORE GOING TO BED...
UM, THIS IS MY FIRST TIME HERE.
KIDS THESE DAYS, THEY DON'T LISTEN TO ADULTS. IT'S A BIG PROBLEM...
...FIRST TIME MEETING YOU, TOO.
AND ALWAYS TALKING BACK...
WAIT!!!
JUMP
WH-WHAT DID YOU JUST SAY? THIS IS YOUR FIRST TIME HERE?
BLACK DRESS, POINTY HAIR, UNIMPRESSED EXPRESSION...

WHAT IS HE MUMBLING ABOUT?
YES, IT'S HER. THEN IT IS WORSE THAN I THOUGHT!
YOU SAID YOU HAD A HEADACHE?
YEAH... I DID...
I'LL GIVE YOU SOMETHING TO TAKE AND THEN YOU SHOULD REST. THAT'S WHY YOU'RE HERE, RIGHT?
WHAT KIND OF NURSE DOESN'T LISTEN TO HIS PATIENT?
DID YOU GET IN BIG TROUBLE?
...THE VICE PRINCIPAL...I HEARD IN THE OFFICE EARLIER. IT'S A SMALL SCHOOL, WORD GETS AROUND.
I THINK THERE'S A MISUNDERSTANDING... I...
YEAH, YEAH...YOU DON'T REMEMBER, RIGHT?

SOMETIMES AFTER A BIG TRAUMA THERE CAN BE SHORT-TERM MEMORY LOSS.
IT'S CALLED SHOCK.
BLAH
BLAH
BLAH
BLAH
LOOK AT THAT HAIR! OBVIOUSLY HE CAN'T SEE STRAIGHT!
YESTERDAY YOU PASSED OUT IN THE EXHIBIT ROOM, ALMOST BROKE A VASE, AND ON TOP OF THAT, HURT YOUR HEAD...
TALK ABOUT MAJOR BAD LUCK...
I USUALLY DON'T LOSE A WAR OF WORDS, BUT THIS GUY IS SOMETHING ELSE!
MISTER!
YES? WHAT? DOES YOUR HEAD HURT AGAIN?
NEVER MIND. IF I GET HIM TALKING AGAIN, HE'LL NEVER STOP!
OH MY, YOU HAVE A HEADACHE, AND I JUST KEEP ON TALKING! I'M SORRY!

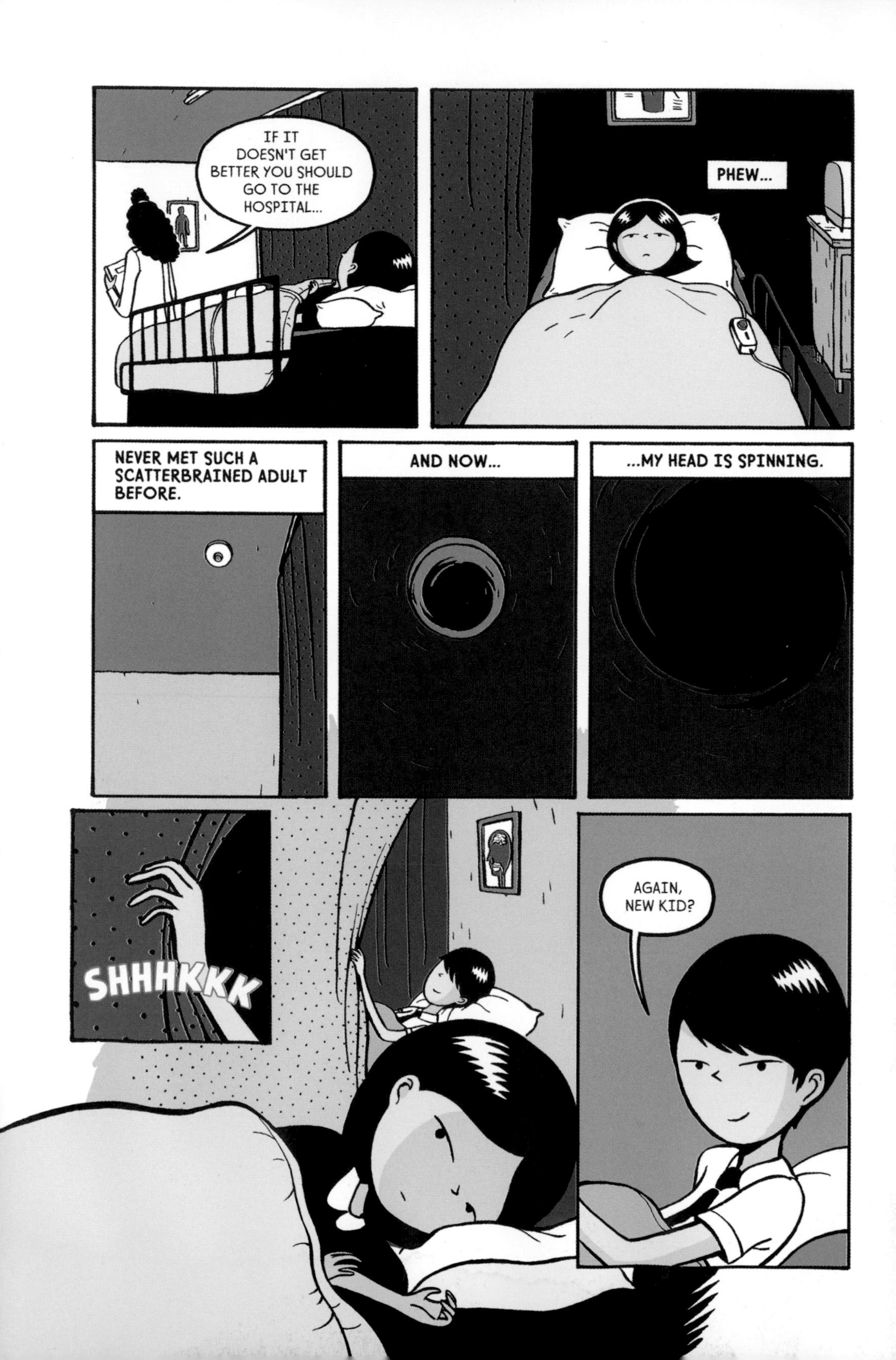
IF IT DOESN'T GET BETTER YOU SHOULD GO TO THE HOSPITAL...
PHEW...
NEVER MET SUCH A SCATTERBRAINED ADULT BEFORE.
AND NOW...
...MY HEAD IS SPINNING.
SHHHKKK
AGAIN, NEW KID?

YOU... KNOW ME?
WE MET HERE YESTERDAY. DON'T YOU REMEMBER?
YOU MUST BE MISTAKEN. LIKE HIM.
ARE YOU TWINS THEN?
SAME HAIR, SAME CLOTHES, SAME FACE?
TW...TWIN?
HE SAW ME YESTERDAY? I DON'T REMEMBER AT ALL. I NEVER CAME HERE.
THEY'RE GETTING SOMETHING WRONG!

NO. THE PERSON I SAW YESTERDAY...IS DEFINITELY YOU!
I HAVE A GREAT MEMORY.
WELL, SO DO I!
THIS MUST BE ABOUT PARTIAL MEMORY LOSS! I READ IT IN A BOOK!
THAT'S ENOUGH!
RIGHT, SORRY! LIKE HE SAID, I'M SURE IT'S ONLY TEMPORARY. YOU'LL BE FINE!
HYUNWOO, GO BACK TO CLASS!
AH, THE GRIM REAPER CALLS. BACK TO THE UNDERWORLD...
BYE, NEW KID! NEXT TIME DON'T IGNORE ME!

LATER THAT NIGHT.
WHAT A MESS...
A TOTAL WRECK...
RAMEN
BISCUIT
SHADOWS COMING TO LIFE, BEING TREATED LIKE AN AMNESIAC...
TWO DAYS AT MY NEW SCHOOL AND ALREADY STRANGE THINGS ARE HAPPENING.
THE ONE GOOD THING IS...

IT'S A REAL UNCOMFORTABLE FEELING.

DAD, CAN WE TALK?
BOY, AM I TIRED. SURE, WHAT'S GOING ON?
IT'S GOING TO BE HARD TO BELIEVE.
THIS MORNING, THERE WAS A SHADOW...
I SEE, I SEE.
SUEE, CAN YOU PICK UP MY CLOTHES FROM THE CLEANERS?
I ASKED THEM TO DELIVER THE CLOTHES, BUT THEY COULDN'T.
BISCUIT
YOU COULD HAVE PICKED THEM UP ON THE WAY.
I TOTALLY FORGOT. THERE'S AN IMPORTANT MEETING TOMORROW.
AT THIS HOUR?
THEY ARE STILL OPEN. PLEASE? IT'S RIGHT AROUND THE CORNER
SHUFFLE
SHUFFLE
WHAT DID I EXPECT? TSK. I KNEW I COULDN'T COUNT ON HIM!

SO ANNOYING!
WHAT KIND OF FATHER MAKES HIS DAUGHTER RUN AN ERRAND AT NIGHT?
WHERE ARE YOU GOING?
HOW LONG HAS SHE BEEN THERE?
YOU SPOOKED ME! CAN'T YOU GIVE ME A WARNING?
A WARNING? HOW? I DON'T EVEN CONTROL IT MYSELF.
ARE YOU SAYING I MADE YOU APPEAR OR SOMETHING?
YES! IT'S ALL YOUR FAULT!
WHEN I HEAR YOUR ANNOYED VOICE, I CAN'T HELP IT!
SO... MY VOICE IS ANNOYING? FINE. I'LL JUST SHUT UP. HOPE YOU HAVE FUN ALONE.
YOU'RE REALLY NOT SPEAKING?
THAT'S WHAT I SAID.
HA! YOU JUST SPOKE!
SIGH

OUTSKIRTS CLEANER
YOU SEE THE CLEANERS? I'M PICKING UP DAD'S CLOTHES.
IF YOU SAY A WORD, I'LL NEVER SPEAK TO YOU AGAIN, OK?
SHH!
THERE'S A RIP RIGHT HERE!
WASN'T THAT THERE WHEN YOU BROUGHT IT IN?
ARE YOU SAYING I'M LYING?
NO, NOT THAT...
I'M VERY SORRY...
I THOUGHT I COULD TRUST THE LOCAL CLEANERS...
OPEN
I'LL BRING THE RECEIPT TOMORROW. I EXPECT A FULL REFUND!
WHOOSH

SORRY TO KEEP YOU WAITING. WHICH HOUSE DID YOU SAY?
BETWEEN HOUSE.
OH, YOU'RE THE KID IN BETWEEN HOUSE. WAIT ONE MOMENT.
SOMEONE YOU KNOW?
SHH! SHUT UP!
YOU SAID IT WOULD BE READY BY TODAY!
YES, BUT WE'RE BEHIND ON ORDERS... I'M SORRY, MRS. HAN, I'M SORRY...
SHE KEEPS LOOKING AT YOU.

OUTSKIRTS CLEANERS
ISN'T SHE IN YOUR CLASS?
WILL YOU BE QUIET? I NEED TO CHECK THESE.
LOOK AT HER.
OUTSKIRTS CLEANERS
I SAID, ISN'T SHE IN YOUR CLASS?
WHAT ARE YOU TALKING ABOUT?
SHE KEPT LOOKING AT YOU EARLIER!

DRAT! WHY IS IT SO DARK? WHY SO FEW STREETLIGHTS?
IT'S 'CAUSE WE'RE IN OUTSKIRTSVILLE.
OTHER NEIGHBORHOODS ARE DIFFERENT?
BUSTLE STREET IS ALWAYS BRIGHT BECAUSE OF THE STREET SIGNS!
IT MUST BE NICE TO LIVE THERE.
SOMEONE'S COMING...

WHY ARE YOU HIDING ME? CAN'T YOU JUST SHOW ME AROUND WITHOUT HIDING?
SO I CAN BE ON THE NEWS OR THE INTERNET?
YOU'LL BE FAMOUS!
I DON'T WANT OTHERS TO GOSSIP ABOUT ME. I'M GOING TO BECOME A REPORTER, BREAKING BIG STORIES WHEN I GROW UP.
BUT YOU COULD BE THE BIG STORY YOURSELF! PRETTY COOL!
FORGET IT. AT MOST I'LL BE "THE SHADOW GIRL."

THEN HOW ABOUT TAKING PICTURES OF ME AND SELLING THEM?
WE COULD MAKE LOTS OF MONEY AND BUY MORE STREETLIGHTS!
I SAID FORGET IT.
AND WHY WOULD I WANT MORE STREETLIGHTS ANYWAY?
I COULD ALWAYS...
YOU COULD ALWAYS WHAT? WHY ARE YOU QUIET ALL OF A SUDDEN?!
DID SHE DISAPPEAR AGAIN?

3.
FOUND MEMORIES

IT'S ALREADY BEEN A WEEK SINCE I TRANSFERRED TO OUTSKIRTS ELEMENTARY. I'M ADJUSTING OK.
EXCEPT FOR ONE THING: MY SHADOW IS ALIVE!
BUT DESPITE MY WORRIES, SHE DOESN'T ACTUALLY CAUSE ANY TROUBLE AT SCHOOL. SHE'S JUST A SHADOW, SO IF THERE'S NO LIGHT, SHE'S NOT EVEN THERE...
THE VICE PRINCIPAL SAID TO SEE HIM IN THE OFFICE.
...OTHER THAN BEING CHATTY, SHE CAN'T REALLY DO MUCH.
THE VICE PRINCIPAL... WHY?
HOW SHOULD I KNOW?
DID I DO SOMETHING WRONG?
AND IF YOU THINK ABOUT IT...
...IT'S NOT BAD TO HAVE MY OWN LITTLE SECRET TO KEEP ME OCCUPIED DURING THE BORING DAYS AT SCHOOL. IT'S EVEN A LITTLE EXCITING.

THAT'S THE GIRL WHO MOVED INTO BETWEEN HOUSE.
WHAT'S WITH HER CLOTHES? SHE GOING TO A FUNERAL?
THEY DON'T KNOW HOW SOPHISTICATED BLACK IS.
A BLACK SUIT?
CLACK
CLACK
HELLO.
FOR A TEACHER HERE, SHE SEEMS TO HAVE GOOD TASTE. WHO IS SHE?
WHAT A PRETTY DRESS.
HELLO PRINCIPAL!
SO THERE IS SOMEONE WHO UNDERSTANDS MY FASHION, EVEN IN THIS SCHOOL.
OH, WHAT A PRETTY T-SHIRT. THOSE ARE PRETTY SNEAKERS, TOO!
NEVER MIND. OF COURSE NOT. WHAT DID I EXPECT? IT'S OUTSKIRTS ELEMENTARY. EVEN THE PRINCIPAL IS PRETTY LAME.

MEANWHILE...
RIGHT NOW THERE ARE FEWER STUDENTS THAN WE ANTICIPATED. I'LL FIND A WAY TO QUICKLY FILL THE REST...
YES...OF COURSE...
SPAP
GRRRR...
CAN'T YOU MOVE ANY FASTER?
WHERE ARE THEY MOVING THOSE DESKS TO?

LOOKS LIKE THE SIDE BUILDING?
MY MOM WAS RIGHT!
WHAT DID YOUR MOM SAY?
YOU ALL KNOW THAT MY MOM KNOWS ABOUT EVERYTHING THAT HAPPENS AT THIS SCHOOL!
BECAUSE SHE'S BEEN PRESIDENT OF THE PTA FOR SIX YEARS AND SHE'S FRIENDS WITH ALL THE TEACHERS, TOO!
YEAH, SO?
ALWAYS "MY MOM THIS" AND "MY MOM THAT"...
SHE SAYS THEY'RE MAKING AN AFTER-SCHOOL CLASS.
AFTER-SCHOOL CLASS?
EXTRACURRICULARS?
NOPE! THE ZERO CLASS!

W-WHAT? ZERO CLASS?
YOU KNOW WHAT ELSE MY MOM SAID?
WHAT?
IT LOOKS LIKE THE VICE PRINCIPAL WILL TEACH THE AFTER-SCHOOL CLASS HIMSELF!
OMG...
THOSE KIDS ARE GOING TO BE MISERABLE!
ISN'T IT WEIRD, THOUGH? THE V.P. DOESN'T KNOW ABOUT "IT."
WHAT DOESN'T THE V.P. KNOW?
DOES IT MATTER WHAT THE V.P. KNOWS OR NOT? I'M TELLING YOU, THE KIDS IN OUR CLASS ARE GOING THERE!
KIDS WHO DROP THE CLASS AVERAGE, LIKE HIM!
AND...
ESPECIALLY HER!
IS SHE POINTING AT ME?

AH, YEJIN KANG AGAIN. WALKS AROUND WITH HER NOSE HIGH, ALWAYS FOLLOWED BY HER TWO LACKEYS.

EVERY CLASS HAS A GIRL LIKE THIS. WHAT A CLICHÉ.
FINE, BRING AS MUCH BACKUP AS YOU WANT.

THE LIKES OF YOU DON'T MATCH UP TO MY...

HUH? WHAT?

GRAB

"UPON FURTHER ANALYSIS OF YOUR CHILD'S BEHAVIOR AND MENTAL STATE, SHE APPEARS TO HAVE CERTAIN EMOTIONAL AND DEVELOPMENTAL DIFFICULTIES."
"PLEASE SUBMIT A PARTICIPATION SLIP TO ATTEND THE AFTER-SCHOOL CLASS."

WHAT'S THE AFTER-SCHOOL CLASS?
ZERO CLASS, REMEMBER?
THE AFTER-SCHOOL CLASS IS THE ZERO CLASS!
THIS PARENT LETTER IS SAYING THAT HAEUN HERE HAS TO GO TO ZERO CLASS! HEY, GUYS! OUR CLASS NOW HAS A ZERO #2!
ZERO #2?
WHO?
YEJIN...I'M NOT A ZERO...
HAEUN IS A ZERO!
REALLY?
WHAT DO YOU MEAN YOU'RE NOT?!
IT'S RIGHT HERE IN THE LETTER!
YEJIN KANG, WHY IS SHE SO MEAN?

OWW!
BANG!
S-SORRY...
S-SORRY...
SEE? THEY'RE EXACTLY THE SAME!
I'VE HEARD OF LOSERS, GEEKS, NERDS, AND EVERYTHING ELSE, BUT "ZERO" IS A NEW ONE.
HAEUN IS A ZERO?
I'M NOT SURE.
YEJIN SAYS SHE IS.
SHE...DID?
WHAT DOES IT MEAN?
OH WELL, WHATEVER THEY CALL IT, IT MEANS THE SAME THING EVERYWHERE.
HUMILIATED, TREATED WITH CONTEMPT, AND IGNORED...
ONCE A LOSER, ALWAYS A LOSER. YOU CEASE TO EXIST.
BUT IT'S NOT MY PLACE TO DO ANYTHING ABOUT IT. I'M JUST THE NEW KID. I HAVE MY OWN PROBLEMS.
SHE'S A ZERO!
THEY'RE THE SAME!
HAEUN JANG IS ZERO #2!
ZERO...
ZERO...
ZERO...

POW! TAKE THAT!
MOVE! YOU'RE IN MY WAY!
DANG ZERO!
SMACK
WHY WON'T MY BOOK FIT?
FLOP
WHAT'S THAT?
WHO CARES? LET'S GO.
DUH...
DID YOU FINISH THE READING HOMEWORK?

COME ON...
IS THIS YOURS?
HUH? OH...
DID YOU MAKE IT?
YEAH...A PROJECT FROM LAST SEMESTER.
BY YOURSELF?
NO, MY MOM HELPED...
I REMEMBER SEEING MOM SITTING AT THE SEWING MACHINE WHEN I WAS LITTLE.
MATH
I REMEMBER HER MAKING SOMETHING...
WHAT WAS IT?
AND...WHAT DOES THAT HAVE TO DO WITH ANYTHING NOW?
NO WONDER IT LOOKS SO GOOD. HERE!
FOR ME?
YEAH, I DON'T NEED IT ANYMORE.

PUT ALL THE BOOKS TO THE SIDE, THEN EVERYTHING ELSE GOES INTO THE BASKET. THEN YOU'LL HAVE ROOM...
MATH
DID SHE UNDERSTAND EVEN HALF OF WHAT I SAID?
LIKE THIS?
STUFF
STUFF
ARE THEY LOOKING AT ME BECAUSE I SPOKE WITH THE LOSER?
WHISPER
WHISPER
SHOULD I PUT THEM IN THEIR PLACE?
NO, I'M TOO TIRED TODAY.
GOOD LUCK WITH ORGANIZING. SEE YOU AROUND.

SO ANNOYING!
GETTING INVOLVED LIKE THAT...THAT'S NOT LIKE ME!
WHAT'S WRONG?
HELLO? I SAID, WHAT'S WRONG?
HUH? WHEN DID YOU APPEAR?
JUST NOW. SO WHAT'S THE PROBLEM?
HAEUN JANG. FORGET IT. SOMETHING STUPID!
HER? THE GIRL FOLLOWING US? IS SHE HAEUN? THE GIRL FROM THE CLEANERS?
CLEANERS? HAEUN? WHAT ARE YOU TALKING ABOUT?
NO WAY...
...IS SHE...FOLLOWING ME?

YOU MAY THINK THAT WE'RE NOW FRIENDS BECAUSE OF EARLIER...
BUT I JUST GAVE YOU THAT BASKET BECAUSE I HAD ONE EXTRA. THAT'S IT.
BAKERY
I'M NOT DOING THIS BECAUSE HAEUN JANG IS THE CLASS LOSER.
HAVE YOU EVER LISTENED TO PUNK ROCK? HAVE YOU READ DETECTIVE NOVELS? WORKED ON THE STUDENT NEWSPAPER? SEE? WE HAVE NOTHING IN COMMON.
I'M JUST GENTLY LETTING HER KNOW WHAT LEVEL SHE HAS TO BE ON TO BE MY FRIEND.
WHAT'S THE USE?
SHE DOESN'T EVEN UNDERSTAND HALF OF WHAT I'M SAYING.
I'M NOT... FOLLOWING...
BAKERY
THERE... THAT'S MY HOUSE...
HUH?!

OUTSKIRTS CLEANERS
YOU SEE...SO...
I WAS... JUST GOING HOME...
NER
THAT'S WHERE YOU LIVE?
YEAH...
THEN WHY DIDN'T YOU JUST SAY YOU WERE GOING HOME?
I'M SORRY...
NO, IN THIS CASE I SHOULD BE APOLOGIZING. IT WAS MY MISTAKE.
ALWAYS CLAIM YOUR MISTAKES. ALWAYS APOLOGIZE IMMEDIATELY.
BUT *YOU*...
HUH...?
...WHAT ARE YOU DOING?!
PAUSE

ARE YOU HIDING BECAUSE OF THE SHADOW?
SH-SHADOW?
I SAW IT WHEN YOU CAME TO PICK UP YOUR CLOTHES LAST NIGHT...
S-SAW WHAT?
YOU WERE TALKING WITH YOUR SHADOW.
SHE SAW THE SHADOW?
WHAT IF SHE TELLS THE OTHERS?! SHOULD I TELL HER THE TRUTH AND ASK HER TO KEEP IT A SECRET?!
NO. DENY!
SHE'S THE CLASS LOSER. NOBODY WILL BELIEVE A WORD SHE SAYS.
HOW CAN I SPEAK TO MY SHADOW? ANYWAYS, IT'S PRETTY HOT THESE DAYS. DID YOU KNOW YOU CAN SEE THINGS IF YOU GET A HEAT STROKE?
HUH?
AREN'T YOU GOING TO GO?
HUH?
I THINK YOUR MOM'S CALLING.
OUTSKIRTS CLEANERS
PHEW...

WHAT DID YOU DO TO HAEUN'S SHADOW?
I DON'T KNOW WHAT YOU MEAN. WHERE DID HAEUN GO?
I SENT HER HOME. SHE WAS A TOTAL PAIN. SHE'S NOT VERY BRIGHT.
I'M WARNING YOU, BE CAREFUL IN FRONT OF OTHERS.
WHY DID YOU SEND HER AWAY? I LIKE PEOPLE LIKE HER. LIKE HAEUN.
THE CLASS LOSER? WHAT FOR?
YOU'RE ALWAYS SO ALONE. IT'S NO FUN. AND YOU HAVE NO FRIENDS.
THIS SCHOOL IS JUST NOT ON MY LEVEL. I CAN'T MAKE FRIENDS WITH LAME PEOPLE.

LOSER! TOTAL LOSER! COMPLETE LOSER!
WH-WHAT? WHY AM I THE LOSER, TOTAL LOSER, COMPLETE LOSER?
YOU HAVE NO FRIENDS AND YOU'RE ALWAYS TALKING TO YOURSELF. ISN'T THAT A LOSER?
I DON'T HAVE FRIENDS BECAUSE I HAVE PRINCIPLES, OK? I HAVE STANDARDS!
THERE'S A DIFFERENCE BETWEEN BEING A LOSER AND NOT HAVING FRIENDS BY CHOICE!
IT'S THE SAME IN THE END... YOU DON'T HAVE ANY FRIENDS!
WAIT A MINUTE...
WHAT MY SHADOW SAID JUST NOW...

I'VE HEARD IT BEFORE!
WHAT'S... WRONG?
THAT'S PRETTY CREEPY...
MAYBE IF I HEAR IT AGAIN IT WILL JOG MY MEMORY.
SAY THAT AGAIN.
WHAT?
"YOU DON'T HAVE ANY FRIENDS."
NO! WHAT AM I, A RECORDER?
IT WAS A STRANGE VOICE.
THE VOICE TEASED ME FOR HAVING NO FRIENDS AND SAID SHE WOULD BE MY FRIEND!
BUT SOMETHING'S WEIRD...
THE WORDS AND VOICE ARE STUCK IN MY HEAD NOW, BUT I CAN'T PUT A FACE TO THEM.
NOT EVEN THE SLIGHTEST...

I SAID, NO!
"YOU DON'T HAVE ANY FRIENDS..."
"YOU DON'T HAVE ANY FRIENDS..."
THAT'S RIGHT! MY FIRST DAY!
AFTER SEEING MY NEW HOMEROOM TEACHER, I REMEMBER A VOICE STOPPING ME.
...BUT WHEN I TURNED AROUND, THERE WAS ONLY A DOOR, SLIGHTLY OPEN.
D-DOOR?
LISTEN, I HAVE PRETTY GOOD HEARING, OK?
ANY SOUND THAT I HEAR IS FILED DEEP IN MY MEMORY.
AND IT COMES BACK TO MY HEAD IF THERE'S A TRIGGER.
YOU JUST TRIGGERED MY MEMORY!
WHAT ARE YOU TALKING ABOUT?
I'M GOING TO FIND OUT WHAT YOU'RE HIDING.

4.
ZERO CLASS
STRONG

THE TRUTH WAS RIGHT UNDER MY NOSE THE WHOLE TIME.
THE VOICE THAT CALLED TO ME FROM THE EXHIBIT ROOM THAT DAY...
IT BELONGED TO MY SHADOW.
WHAT'S GOING ON?
WHAT THE HECK HAPPENED THAT DAY IN THE EXHIBIT ROOM?
YOU...DON'T REMEMBER?
THAT'S NOT WHAT I SAID.
I WANT TO HEAR YOUR VERSION.
ANSWER MY QUESTION!
GRIN
WHY ARE YOU SMILING?

WHAT ARE YOU HIDING? HUH?
HEY!
WHY DON'T YOU TELL ME THE TRUTH ALREADY? WHAT HAPPENED THAT DAY?
I CAN'T REALLY REMEMBER EITHER.
I WOKE UP AND THIS WAS ME. THAT'S IT. I'M JUST AS STUMPED.
ONE DAY YOU JUST CAME INTO EXISTENCE. THAT'S YOUR STORY?
YOU MUST THINK I'M REALLY STUPID!
WHAT CAN I SAY?
IF THE SHOE FITS.
EXHIBIT ROOM
WITH THAT, MY SHADOW DISAPPEARED. THIS TIME, THOUGH, I FELT LIKE SHE WENT AWAY ON PURPOSE.
EVEN WEIRDER, UNFORTUNATELY...

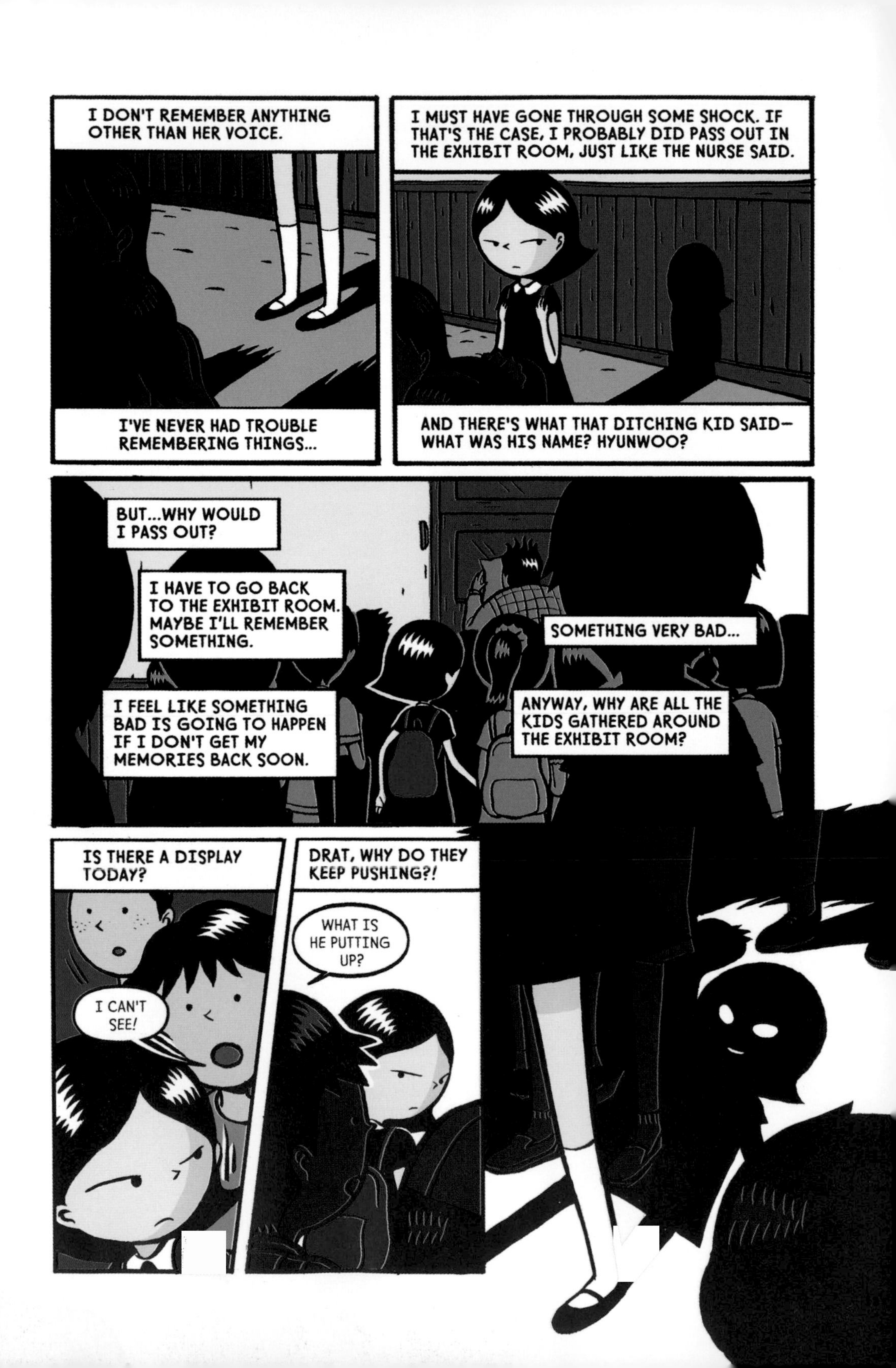
I DON'T REMEMBER ANYTHING OTHER THAN HER VOICE.
I'VE NEVER HAD TROUBLE REMEMBERING THINGS...
I MUST HAVE GONE THROUGH SOME SHOCK. IF THAT'S THE CASE, I PROBABLY DID PASS OUT IN THE EXHIBIT ROOM, JUST LIKE THE NURSE SAID.
AND THERE'S WHAT THAT DITCHING KID SAID—WHAT WAS HIS NAME? HYUNWOO?
BUT...WHY WOULD I PASS OUT?
I HAVE TO GO BACK TO THE EXHIBIT ROOM. MAYBE I'LL REMEMBER SOMETHING.
I FEEL LIKE SOMETHING BAD IS GOING TO HAPPEN IF I DON'T GET MY MEMORIES BACK SOON.
SOMETHING VERY BAD...
ANYWAY, WHY ARE ALL THE KIDS GATHERED AROUND THE EXHIBIT ROOM?
IS THERE A DISPLAY TODAY?
I CAN'T SEE!
DRAT, WHY DO THEY KEEP PUSHING?!
WHAT IS HE PUTTING UP?

I HATE BIG CROWDS.
I NEED TO GET OUT OF HERE!
BUSTLE
BUSTLE
THIS IS SO ANNOYING!
POKE
POKE
POOOOKE
YOU LITTLE RATS!

MURMUR MURMUR
WHY ARE YOU LITTLE RATS SQUEAKING ABOUT BEHIND MY BACK?!
GET OUT OF THE WAY!
JUDGING BY THE CAVEMAN-LIKE LANGUAGE AND FACE...
LOOKS LIKE SOMEONE I SHOULD AVOID IF POSSIBLE!
YOU AGAIN?
WH-WHAT IS GOING ON HERE?!

I'M TOO BUSY TO BE WASTING MY TIME ON STUFF LIKE THIS!
POKE
ON SOME LITTLE...
...DELINQUENT.
YOU KNOW, RATS THAT LIVE IN TALL BUILDINGS ARE THE SNEAKIEST KIND.
I'M NOT A RAT!
AND YOU...SHOWING YOUR LITTLE NOSE HERE...AFTER THAT SHOW YOU PUT ON, FAINTING IN THE EXHIBIT ROOM?
SPARK SPARK
THIS TIME I'LL REALLY TEACH YOU A LESSON...
VICE PRINCIPAL, THE NURSE IS LOOKING FOR YOU!
IF I SEE YOU SNIFFING AROUND THE EXHIBIT ROOM AGAIN, I WON'T BE SO EASY ON YOU NEXT TIME!

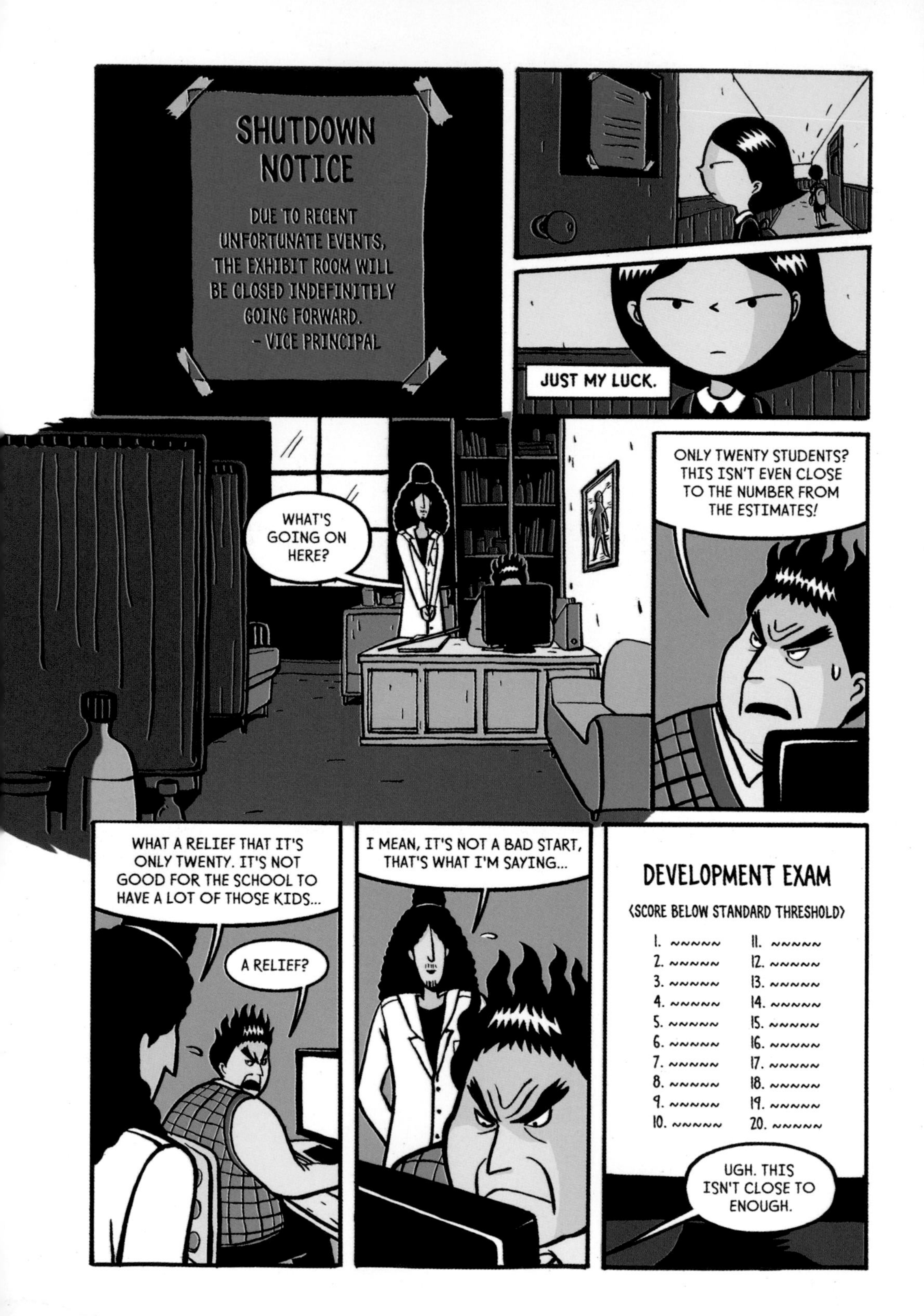
SHUTDOWN NOTICE
DUE TO RECENT UNFORTUNATE EVENTS, THE EXHIBIT ROOM WILL BE CLOSED INDEFINITELY GOING FORWARD.
- VICE PRINCIPAL
JUST MY LUCK.
WHAT'S GOING ON HERE?
ONLY TWENTY STUDENTS? THIS ISN'T EVEN CLOSE TO THE NUMBER FROM THE ESTIMATES!
WHAT A RELIEF THAT IT'S ONLY TWENTY. IT'S NOT GOOD FOR THE SCHOOL TO HAVE A LOT OF THOSE KIDS...
A RELIEF?
I MEAN, IT'S NOT A BAD START, THAT'S WHAT I'M SAYING...
DEVELOPMENT EXAM
<SCORE BELOW STANDARD THRESHOLD>
1. ~~~~~
2. ~~~~~
3. ~~~~~
4. ~~~~~
5. ~~~~~
6. ~~~~~
7. ~~~~~
8. ~~~~~
9. ~~~~~
10. ~~~~~
11. ~~~~~
12. ~~~~~
13. ~~~~~
14. ~~~~~
15. ~~~~~
16. ~~~~~
17. ~~~~~
18. ~~~~~
19. ~~~~~
20. ~~~~~
UGH. THIS ISN'T CLOSE TO ENOUGH.

CREEEAAAAAK
WHY IS THIS DOOR CLOSED?
CONFIRMED—THERE'S NO ONE ELSE IN THE BATHROOM!

I NEED TO TALK WITH MY SHADOW AGAIN.
WHEN YOU THINK ABOUT IT, SHE ONLY APPEARED AT CERTAIN MOMENTS. I NEED TO FIGURE OUT WHAT THEY WERE.
THOSE MOMENTS...
SO ANNOYING! WHAT KIND OF FATHER MAKES HIS DAUGHTER RUN AN ERRAND AT NIGHT?
SO ANNOYING! GETTING INVOLVED LIKE THAT...THAT'S NOT LIKE ME!
THAT'S IT!
YES! IT'S ALL YOUR FAULT!
WHEN I HEAR YOUR ANNOYED VOICE, I CAN'T HELP IT!
I CAN MAKE HER APPEAR IF I GET ANNOYED!

SO HOW DO I BECOME ANNOYED?
BE ANNOYED...
BE ANNOYED...
TURN
BE ANNOYED...
STARE
BE ANNOYED...
BE ANNOYED...
AH, SO ANNOYING! WHERE THE HECK IS SHE?
STOP! YOU'LL SCREAM MY EARS OFF!
THAT'S WEIRD. YOU LOOK A LITTLE PLEASED TO SEE ME.
SUCCESS!

YEAH, I CALLED FOR YOU. FROM NOW ON, HURRY UP WHENEVER YOUR OWNER CALLS!
MY...OWNER?
WHO ELSE? ME! YOU'RE MY SHADOW!
WOW, WHAT AM I, SOME KIND OF PET?
ANYWAYS, I DON'T THINK THAT'S REALLY WHY YOU CALLED FOR ME.
THAT'S RIGHT. THERE'S A REASON WHY I CALLED YOU. I WANT TO FINISH OUR CONVERSATION FROM YESTERDAY.
THERE'S NOTHING MORE TO SAY. I TOLD YOU, I DON'T REMEMBER EITHER! JUST LIKE YOU!
THAT'S NOT WHAT I WANT TO TALK ABOUT.
HUH? THEN WHAT?

HAEUN'S SHADOW!
HA-HAEUN'S SHADOW?
WHAT DID YOU DO TO HAEUN'S SHADOW YESTERDAY?
I SAW YOU GRABBING HER SHADOW!
WHAT ARE YOU TALKING ABOUT?
WHERE'S SEOYEON? I HAVEN'T SEEN HER.
HER TEACHER SENT HER TO THE FACULTY OFFICE. SHE'S STILL THERE.
SHE'S AT THE OFFICE?
WE'LL TALK LATER...!
IS SEOYEON HAN GOING TO ZERO CLASS, TOO?
SEOYEON? WHY HER? SHE'S NOT A ZERO.
OH WOW, YOU DIDN'T KNOW? IT'S NOT JUST ZEROES THAT GO TO ZERO CLASS.
HUH?
EVERYONE WITH LOW SCORES FROM LAST SEMESTER'S DEVELOPMENT EXAM WILL BE GOING!
WHAT?

THAT'S NONSENSE! HOW CAN THEY FIND ZEROS THROUGH A STUPID TEST?
WHY NOT? THE REAL CRAZY THING IS, I HEARD THERE'S NOT ENOUGH KIDS IN THE ZERO CLASS.
THE V.P. IS GOING BERSERK BECAUSE OF THAT.
WHY NOT JUST GO AFTER KIDS WHO DIDN'T TAKE THE EXAM INSTEAD? YOU KNOW, LIKE TRANSFER KIDS, LIKE SUEE LEE.
SHE'S THE ONLY TRANSFER STUDENT THIS YEAR.
STILL! THE ZERO CLASS IS PERFECT FOR THAT CREEPY GIRL, HA HA HA!
I'LL TELL THE V.P. TO MAKE HER TAKE THE TEST!
WHY IS THE SHADOW MOVING?
STAY STILL!
DID YOU...
...JUST HEAR SOMETHING?
NO, NOTHING.

NO, I DEFINITELY HEARD A NOISE!
THERE MUST BE SOMEONE ELSE HERE!
WHO CARES?
IT'S A SECRET!
WHAT'S A SECRET?
YEJIN! HURRY!
WHAT THE HECK? SEOYEON MUST REALLY BE GOING TO ZERO CLASS.
HYUNWOO...
HYUNWOO'S BEING SENT TO ZERO CLASS!
WHAT?
HA! HYUNWOO?! THAT'S WHAT YOU GET FOR DITCHING CLASS.
SEOYEON! THAT MAKES NO SENSE! HE'S THE BEST STUDENT IN CLASS!
IT'S TRUE! I JUST HEARD IN THE FACULTY OFFICE!
THE MIGHTY TOP STUDENT, FALLEN FROM GRACE!
OUT OF MY WAY!

THAT'S HYUNWOO'S VOICE!
LET'S CHECK IT OUT!
HURRY UP!
RUN
CREEEAAK
NOW, LET'S CONTINUE OUR CONVERSATION!
I TOLD YOU, THAT'S IT!
SO I HEARD YOU CAME IN LAST IN THE EXAM?
AREN'T YOU CURIOUS, TOO? LET'S GO OUTSIDE!
IT'S NONE OF YOUR BUSINESS!
MOVE!

SEE, WHATEVER YOU DO, IT'S SO ANNOYING!
EVEN WHEN YOU COME IN LAST, YOU PUT ON THIS BIG SHOW! TURNING IN A BLANK TEST SHEET!
YOU THINK A STUNT LIKE THAT WILL MAKE YOUR PARENTS COME BACK FOR YOU?
HYUNWOO'S PARENTS LEFT HIM?
WHAT DID YOU SAY?
JUST TRY AND HIT ME!
YOU THINK I WON'T?
UH...

BYUNGTAE! HYUNWOO!
STOP RIGHT THIS INSTANT!
YOU LITTLE...

WHERE IS THE MUSIC ROOM?
THAT KID...
WHAT A FREAK...
HOW LONG HAS SHE BEEN THERE?
SHE'S A ZERO!
MUSIC ROOM...
I CALLED HER A ZERO BEFORE I COULD STOP MYSELF!
IS IT CONTAGIOUS?
WAA, GO AWAY!
WHERE IS IT?
YOU KNOW, I NEVER NOTICED, BUT...
ON CLOSER INSPECTION, THESE KIDS ARE DIFFERENT THAN THE LOSERS IN MY OTHER SCHOOL.
THEIR FACES...THEIR VOICES...IT'S ALL VERY...VACANT!
WHERE IS THE MUSIC ROOM?

YOU LITTLE RATS! WHAT ARE YOU DOING HERE?!
GRR... IF SCHOOL IS OVER...
...DON'T YOU HAVE SOMEWHERE BETTER TO BE?
MURMUR
MURMUR
THAT'S RIGHT...HURRY ON NOW...
RUMBLE
HMM, I SEE A RAT WHO APPARENTLY HAS NO AFTER-SCHOOL ACTIVITIES?
GRIN
NOT AGAIN...

WHAT IS HE GOING TO FREAK OUT ABOUT THIS TIME?
GLANCE
GLIDE
HUH? NOT ME?
TODAY'S TARGET IS THE ZERO. SORRY, ZERO.
YOU DON'T HAVE ANYTHING AFTER SCHOOL, HUH?
WELL, THANKS TO HER I WON'T HAVE TO DEAL WITH A STUPID SITUATION.
THERE'S A PERFECT CLASS FOR YOUR LEVEL...
WHY IS HE SMILING LIKE THAT?
GRIN
WHERE IS THE MUSIC ROOM?
THAT'S RIGHT, I'LL SHOW YOU. FOLLOW ME...
HE'S NOT TAKING HER TO THE MUSIC ROOM. HE'S TAKING HER TO THE ZERO CLASS!

SO WHAT IS THIS FAMOUS ZERO CLASS?
IT'S A CLASS FOR LOSERS. NO, ZEROES.
FOR KIDS LIKE HAEUN?
THE CLASSROOM EVEN LOOKS LIKE A PRISON. SOMETHING'S FISHY.
I HAVE TO CHECK IT OUT!
WHAT?
THE ZERO CLASS...
WHY?
I WANT TO KNOW WHAT IT IS, WHAT KIDS GO THERE.
YOU SHOWING INTEREST IN OTHER KIDS? THAT'S NEW.
I'M GETTING THIS FEELING. I HAVE TO TAKE A LOOK.

THAT'S HAEUN.
SHE LOOKS DIFFERENT HERE THAN IN THE CLASSROOM.
NO, SHE ACTUALLY LOOKS NORMAL HERE. JUST LOOKS A LITTLE TIRED, THAT'S ALL.
AND HYUNWOO...WELL, HE'S SO CONFIDENT, HE STANDS OUT. AS EXPECTED.
WAIT, THOSE TWO ARE THE ONLY NORMAL ONES!
THE OTHER KIDS ARE ALL REALLY WEIRD!
WEIRD?
THOSE KIDS...
...AREN'T REGULAR LOSERS...
WHAT ARE YOU TALKING ABOUT?

ALL THEIR EYES ARE HOLLOW. LIKE A BUNCH OF MINDLESS ZOMBIES!

5.
THE DREAM

HAEUN!
SUEE?!

WERE YOU...WAITING FOR ME?
I NEED TO ASK YOU A QUESTION.
ME?!
DO YOU REMEMBER WHAT YOU SAID WHEN YEJIN PUSHED YOU THE OTHER DAY?
WHAT I SAID?
YOU SAID YOU'RE NOT A ZERO.

WHAT DOES IT MEAN TO BE A ZERO?
YOU... CAN'T TELL?
OF COURSE I CAN TELL. ZEROES AREN'T LIKE NORMAL KIDS. THEIR EYES ARE HOLLOW AND THEY MUMBLE.
BUT IT'S STRANGE THAT THEY ACT SO WEIRD. DO YOU KNOW WHY, THOUGH?
SO...YOU CAN'T SEE IT.
WHY DOES SHE KEEP AVOIDING THE QUESTION?
I'M NOT ASKING ABOUT HOW THEY LOOK. WHAT I WANT TO KNOW IS WHY THEY BECOME LIKE THAT.
WELL...
ZEROES DON'T HAVE SHADOWS! THAT'S WHY THEY ACT LIKE THAT!
NO... SHADOWS?
WAIT...WHO'S THAT?
HYUNWOO?!

WHAT DO YOU MEAN THEY HAVE NO SHADOWS?!
EXACTLY WHAT I SAID! EVERYONE SHOULD HAVE A SHADOW, BUT ZEROES DON'T!
ZEROES...ARE KIDS WHO DON'T HAVE SHADOWS?
HOW IS THAT EVEN POSSIBLE?
DON'T BELIEVE ME? WHY DON'T YOU TAKE A LOOK FOR YOURSELF TOMORROW AT SCHOOL?
DON'T WORRY. I'LL CONFIRM WITH MY OWN EYES.
SUIT YOURSELF. SEE YA...
WAIT!
YES?

THE ZEROES. DID THEY ALWAYS NOT HAVE SHADOWS?
OF COURSE THEY USED TO HAVE SHADOWS!
THEN HOW DID THE SHADOWS DISAPPEAR?
HMM...
BECOMING A ZERO...IT'S A DISEASE... A DISEASE WHERE YOU LOSE YOUR SHADOW...
IT HAPPENS TO KIDS WHO ARE BULLIED...

DOES THAT MEAN YOU'LL BECOME A ZERO, TOO?
ME... A ZERO?
YOU'RE THE CLASS LOSE- I MEAN, THE KIDS BULLY YOU.
HEY, WATCH WHAT YOU SAY.
NO... SHE'S RIGHT...
THESE DAYS, YEJIN...SHE KEEPS CALLING ME A ZERO...
HAEUN, DON'T WORRY TOO MUCH.
NO ONE KNOWS FOR SURE IF THIS ZERO THING IS A DISEASE...
...PLUS, YOU STILL HAVE YOUR SHADOW.
IF IT'S NOT A DISEASE, THEN WHAT IS IT?
WELL...I DON'T KNOW EITHER.

I WANT TO KNOW MORE!
HOW ABOUT WE INVESTIGATE THESE ZEROES?
NORMALLY, I'D LIKE TO LOOK INTO IT ALONE. BUT I'M NOT FAMILIAR YET WITH THIS SCHOOL. THIS KID, HYUNWOO, LOOKS LIKE HE COULD BE HELPFUL.
INVESTIGATE?
LET'S TRY TO FIND OUT WHY THE SHADOWS DISAPPEAR!
WHERE IS HE GOING?
WHAT GOOD WILL THAT DO?
IF WE CAN FIND THE REASON, THEN MAYBE WE CAN STOP IT!
YOU REALLY THINK SO?
YOU NEVER KNOW!
I'LL THINK ABOUT IT. WELL THEN, SEE YOU LATER...
WHAT? DID HE ACTUALLY BRUSH ME OFF?

CLICK
SO WHAT IF WE LIVE CLOSE TO DAD'S OFFICE? HE'S BUSIER THAN BEFORE!

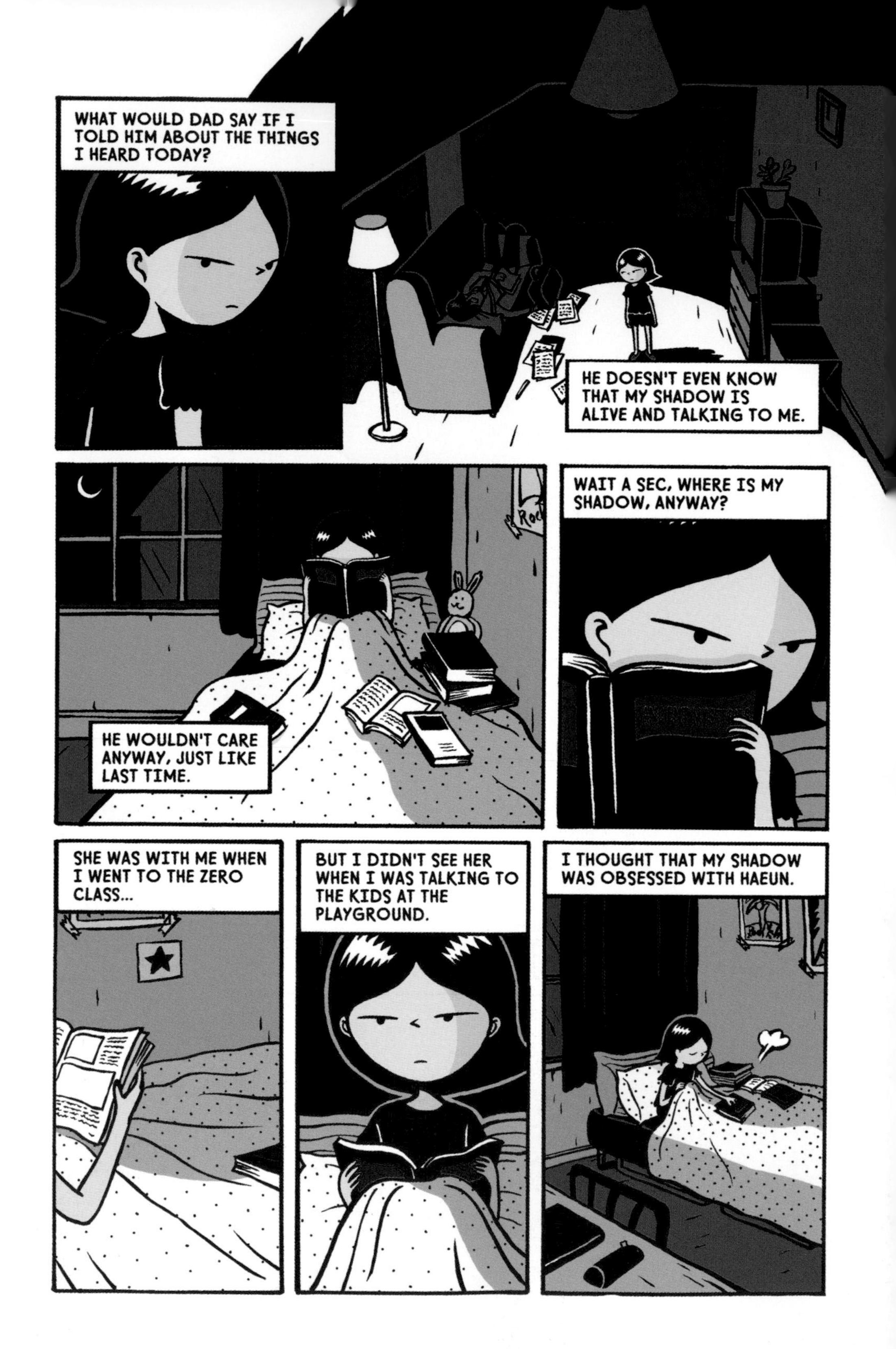
WHAT WOULD DAD SAY IF I TOLD HIM ABOUT THE THINGS I HEARD TODAY?
HE DOESN'T EVEN KNOW THAT MY SHADOW IS ALIVE AND TALKING TO ME.
HE WOULDN'T CARE ANYWAY, JUST LIKE LAST TIME.
WAIT A SEC, WHERE IS MY SHADOW, ANYWAY?
SHE WAS WITH ME WHEN I WENT TO THE ZERO CLASS...
BUT I DIDN'T SEE HER WHEN I WAS TALKING TO THE KIDS AT THE PLAYGROUND.
I THOUGHT THAT MY SHADOW WAS OBSESSED WITH HAEUN.

WELL, SHE WAS LIKE THIS FROM THE BEGINNING.
SHE APPEARED WHEN I GOT ANNOYED, BUT SHE WENT AWAY WHENEVER SHE FELT LIKE IT.
COME TO THINK OF IT, I DON'T KNOW MUCH ABOUT MY SHADOW.
THE PROBLEM IS, I'M TOO HIGH-STRUNG THESE DAYS.
I GET SO EASILY ANNOYED...
TOO CONCERNED ABOUT SILLY LITTLE THINGS.
IS IT BECAUSE OF MY SHADOW?
BECAUSE MY SHADOW IS ALIVE?

I SHOULD BE MORE CAREFUL.
CAN'T LET MY SHADOW CHANGE MY PERSONALITY.
NOT A SHADOW, OF ALL THINGS.
Rock N Roll
ROCK
MYSTERY!

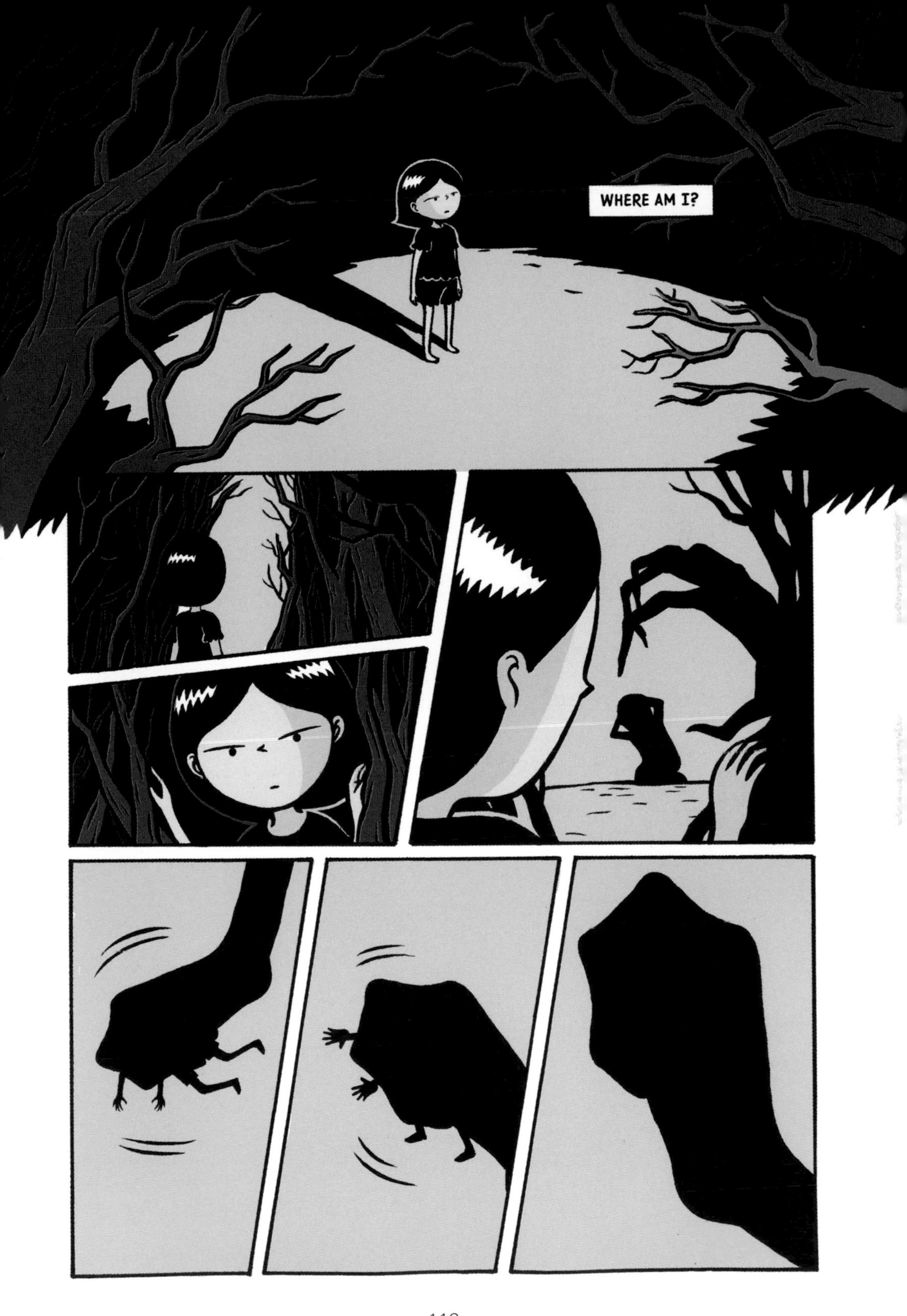
WHERE AM I?

PLEASE
PLEASE
PLEASE
PLEASE
PLEASE
PLEASE

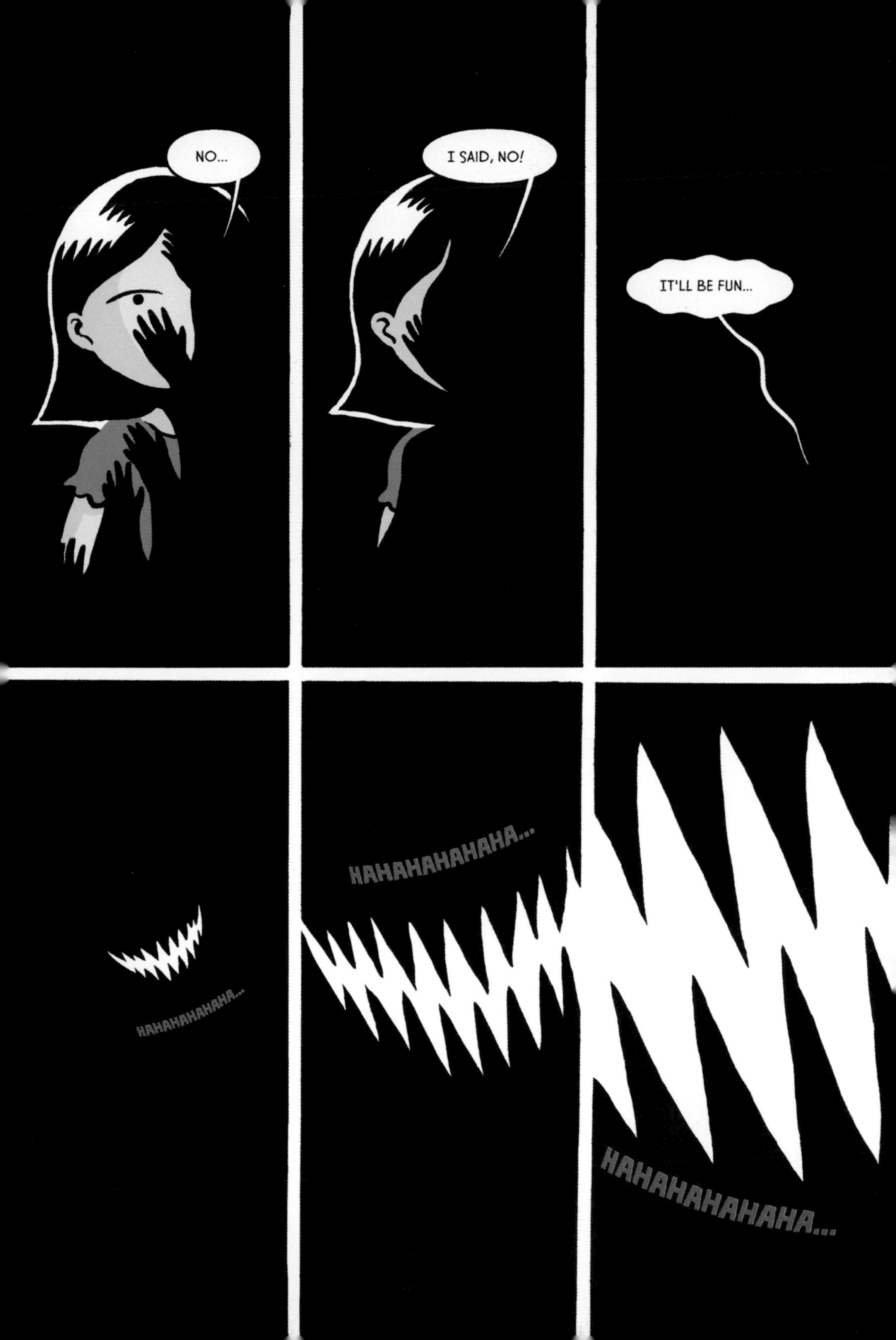
NO...
I SAID, NO!
IT'LL BE FUN...
HAHAHAHAHAHA...
HAHAHAHAHAHA...
HAHAHAHAHAHA...

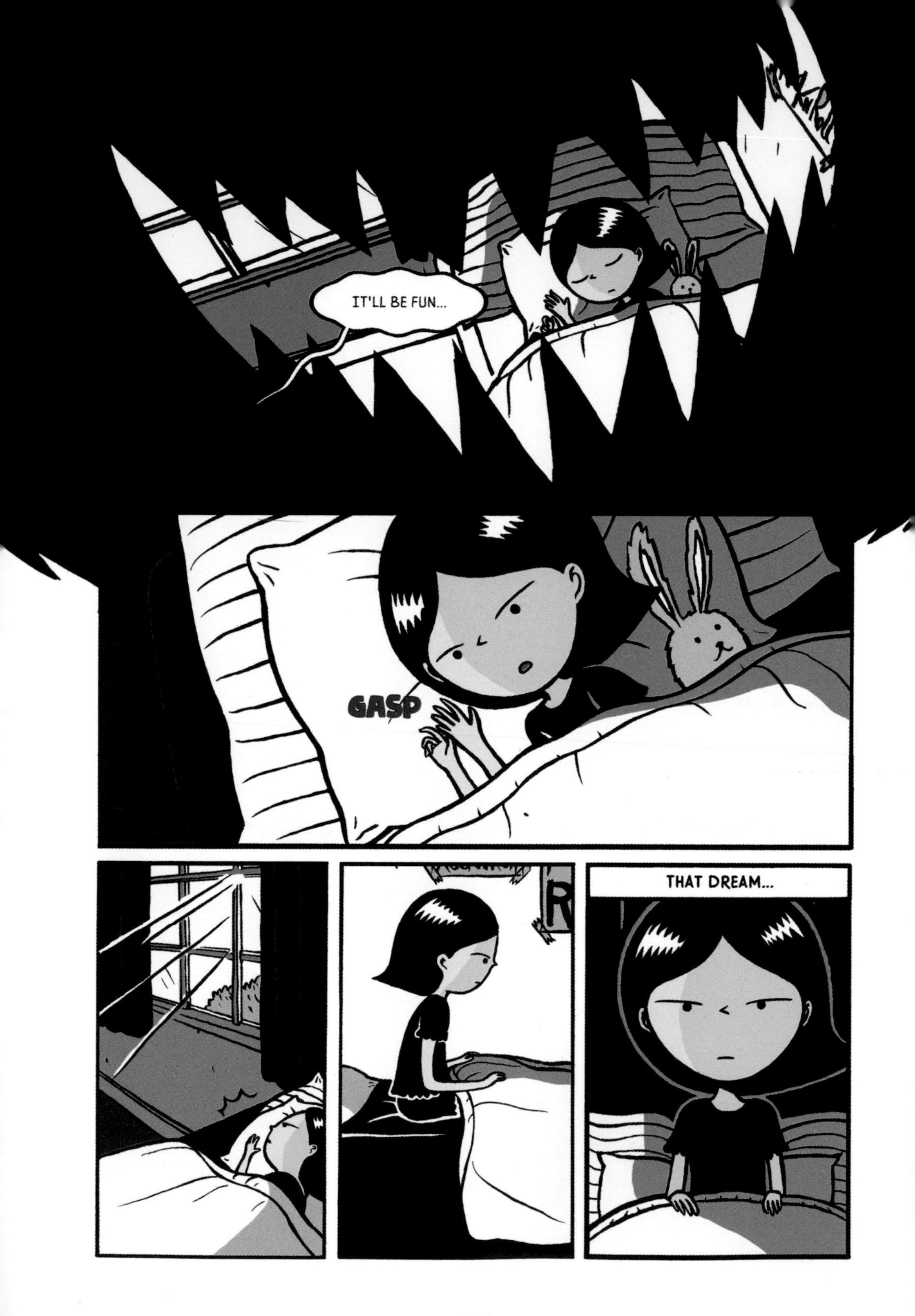
IT'LL BE FUN...
GASP
THAT DREAM...

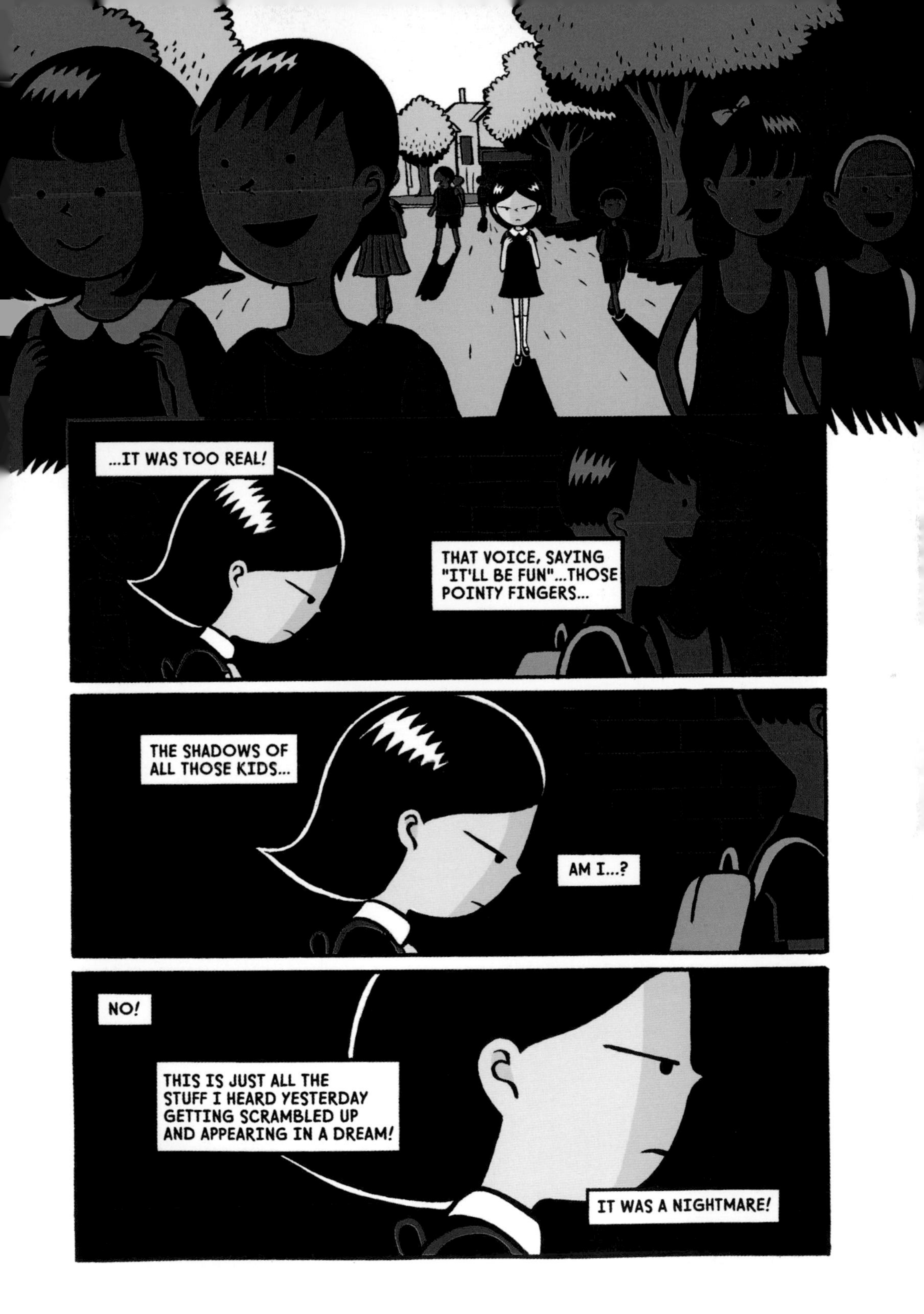
...IT WAS TOO REAL!
THAT VOICE, SAYING "IT'LL BE FUN"...THOSE POINTY FINGERS...
THE SHADOWS OF ALL THOSE KIDS...
AM I...?
NO!
THIS IS JUST ALL THE STUFF I HEARD YESTERDAY GETTING SCRAMBLED UP AND APPEARING IN A DREAM!
IT WAS A NIGHTMARE!

WHATEVER IT WAS, I DIDN'T GET MUCH SLEEP...
I'M TIRED...AND ANNOYED!
HEY, ZERO!
I'M...I'M NOT A ZERO...
WHADDYA MEAN YOU'RE NOT A ZERO? IT'S EXACTLY LOSERS LIKE YOU WHO BECOME ZEROES!
EVERYONE KNOWS THAT, MORON!
OWW!

WHY IS HE STARING AT ME LIKE THAT?
IT'S NOT LIKE I PUSHED HIM!
UM...UH...
IT'S NOT MY FAULT!
FORGET IT. I DON'T WANT MY SHADOW TO COME OUT.
WHOA...
HE...HE REALLY BECAME A ZERO!
RUN AWAY! IT MIGHT BE CONTAGIOUS!
WHAT ARE THEY TALKING ABOUT?

THE KID I JUST SAW...
...SOMETHING'S CHANGED!
HOLLOW EYES...
...NO SHADOW!
WHAT JUST HAPPENED?
WHEN DID HE LOSE HIS SHADOW?

WHAT ON EARTH
IS HAPPENING?

6.
ZERO
DETECTIVE CLUB
GOODNESS, I CAN BARELY SEE THE FLOOR!
DOES THE VICE PRINCIPAL REALLY THINK THIS ROOM CAN BE USED FOR THE AFTER-SCHOOL CLASS?
HE MUST BE IN QUITE A HURRY TO MAKE ME CLEAN THIS ROOM...

HAEUN SAID...
ZEROES HAVE A DISEASE WHERE THEY LOSE THEIR SHADOWS.
AND THAT THEY GET THE DISEASE BY BEING BULLIED.
THAT KID EARLIER WAS BEING BULLIED.
IS THAT WHY HE BECAME A ZERO?
DRAT, I LEFT THE SCENE TOO EARLY AND MISSED THE CRUCIAL MOMENT!
WAIT...I THINK I SAW SOMETHING!
BLAH BLAH... BLAH BLAH...

OUTSKIRTS ELEMENTARY
I NEED TO FIND SOMEWHERE...
WITH LOTS OF SUNLIGHT...
THAT'S ALSO QUIET!
ELEMENTARY
FOCUS...FOCUS...
SUEE LEE?
WHERE IS SHE GOING?

BE ANNOYED...
BE ANNOYED...
BE ANNOYED...
I'M ANNOYED! I'M ANNOYED!
WHAT'S GOING ON?
I HAVE SOMETHING TO ASK YOU!
WHAT COULD IT BE?
I KNOW YOU SAW THAT KID EARLIER!
WHAT ARE YOU TALKING ABOUT?
I DIDN'T WANT TO GET INVOLVED WITH THAT KID, BUT I THINK THAT I SAW YOU, THAT YOU WERE THERE THIS MORNING!

YOU... YOU NOTICED... ME?
YES, SO TELL ME WHAT YOU SAW!
YOU'RE A SHADOW, TOO, SO I KNOW YOU SAW IT WHEN THAT KID LOST HIS SHADOW!
YOU... DIDN'T SEE IT?
WOULD I BE ASKING YOU IF I DID?
WHY DIDN'T YOU?
WHY DIDN'T I? BECAUSE I WAS TOO BUSY NOT WANTING TO BE SEEN IN CASE SHE MIGHT APPEAR.
EXCEPT SHE WAS THERE THE WHOLE TIME!
I DON'T KNOW WHY. JUST TELL ME WHAT YOU SAW. HOW DID IT DISAPPEAR? JUST SLIPPED AWAY?
WHAT ARE YOU STARING AT THE WALL FOR?

WAIT, YOU'RE NOT HIDING, ARE YOU?
YOU SHOULD HIDE BETTER. IT'S NOT MUCH FUN WHEN IT'S SO EASY TO FIND YOU.
ARE YOU DITCHING THE AFTER-SCHOOL CLASS?
CLASS HASN'T STARTED YET. TEACHER SAID HE'D BE A LITTLE LATE, SO WE SHOULD BE READING ON OUR OWN.
SO WHY ARE YOU HERE AND NOT READING IN CLASS?
I CAME TO ANSWER YOUR PROPOSAL, OF COURSE.
MY PROPOSAL?
ALREADY FORGOT ABOUT ASKING ME TO INVESTIGATE THE ZEROES TOGETHER?

WHAT'S WITH THE SUDDEN CHANGE OF HEART? YOU DIDN'T SEEM SO INTERESTED YESTERDAY.
I TOLD YOU THAT I'D THINK ABOUT IT.
TO BE HONEST, I KINDA GOT USED TO THE ZEROES. BUT YESTERDAY, I COULDN'T STOP THINKING ABOUT HOW WORRIED HAEUN WAS.
I FIGURED IT WOULD BE GOOD TO FIND OUT WHAT'S GOING ON AND STOP IT.
HOW ARE YOU GOING TO INVESTIGATE? WHAT'S THE PLAN?
FIRST, WE FOLLOW THEM. SECRETLY.
JUST THE TWO OF US? THERE'S A LOT OF THEM, YOU KNOW.
CAN'T BRING IN ANY OTHERS. TOO HARD TO KEEP IT SECRET IF THERE ARE TOO MANY PEOPLE.
WE COULD USE ONE MORE. SOMEONE WE BOTH KNOW, WHO IS GOOD AT KEEPING SECRETS.
WHERE ARE WE GOING TO FIND SOMEONE LIKE THAT?
RIGHT THERE...
ARE YOU KIDDING?
HAEUN HAS BEEN GOING TO THIS SCHOOL SINCE FIRST GRADE, LIKE ME. SHE'LL BE PERFECT.
HAEUN! COME HERE FOR A SEC!

SUEE AND I FORMED THE ZERO DETECTIVE CLUB, AND WE WANT YOU TO JOIN.
ZERO DETECTIVE CLUB? WHEN DID HE MAKE UP THAT SILLY NAME?
DO YOU REALLY THINK... I CAN HELP?
OF COURSE! THEN IT'S SETTLED. HAEUN, YOU'RE IN THE CLUB.
THE ZERO DETECTIVE CLUB OFFICIALLY LAUNCHES TODAY!

SUEE IS CLUB CAPTAIN. I'M THE MORE NATURAL LEADER, BUT SINCE THE WHOLE THING WAS HER IDEA, I'LL STEP ASIDE!
WHENEVER BOYS GET INVOLVED, THEY ALWAYS WANT TO GIVE OUT RANKS.
NOW GIVE US YOUR ORDERS, CAPTAIN!
WILL YOU STOP CALLING ME THAT?
HOW LONG ARE YOU GOING TO BE STANDING IN THE SHADE, CAPTAIN? IT'S CREEPY.
I DON'T MIND CREEPY!
SUCH WEIRD TASTE.
IS THE SHADOW GONE?
FOCUS! FOCUS! ENOUGH WITH THE CHITCHAT. LET'S CONCENTRATE ON INVESTIGATING THE ZEROES!
ROGER THAT, CAPTAIN!

LET'S GET DOWN TO BUSINESS...
WE'RE GOING TO FOLLOW THE ZEROES...
AND LEARN EVERYTHING WE CAN ABOUT THEM...
THEIR NAMES, THEIR CLASS SCHEDULES...
WHAT THEY DO, WHERE THEY GO, WHO THEIR FRIENDS ARE, THE WHOLE PICTURE.

WHAT ABOUT...GOING TO CLASS?
FIND A WAY TO DITCH.
HOW...?
LOOK AT SUEE. SHE'S AN EXPERT.
IF SHE DOES THE SAME THING, WE MIGHT GET CAUGHT.
GIVE HER A CHANCE.
SHE MIGHT SURPRISE YOU.
YOU ALSO NEED TO SEE THE NURSE?
IS THERE SOMETHING GOING AROUND?

SO WHAT HAVE WE LEARNED?
I'LL GO FIRST. IN FIRST AND SECOND GRADES, THE ZEROES ARE USUALLY THE SMALLER KIDS IN THE CLASS...
...AND THEY ARE LONERS WHO DIDN'T HAVE FRIENDS TO BEGIN WITH.
THERE'S ONE ZERO IN FIRST GRADE, AND TWO IN SECOND GRADE. THAT'S IT.
MY RESULTS ARE SIMILAR: THE ZEROES ARE THE BULLIED KIDS... TWO IN THIRD GRADE... TEN IN FOURTH GRADE...
IT'S THE SAME STORY IN FIFTH AND SIXTH GRADE. THEY'RE THE LONERS IN THE CLASS. ELEVEN IN FIFTH GRADE, THIRTEEN IN SIXTH.
CAPTAIN, WHAT ARE YOU DOING?
SCRRT SCRRT

LOOK.
I DON'T GET IT...
LOOK AT WHERE THE LINE BENDS.
THERE'S A SHARP INCREASE STARTING IN FOURTH GRADE!
12
10
8
6
4
2
0
GRADE 1 GRADE 2 GRADE 3 GRADE 4 GRADE 5 GRADE 6
RIGHT! THERE'S ONLY A FEW ZEROES FROM FIRST TO THIRD GRADE. WHY IS THAT?
NO CLUE.
IS THERE ANYTHING DIFFERENT THAT FOURTH GRADERS HAVE TO DO HERE?
I DON'T THINK SO. THEY DON'T HAVE ANYTHING SPECIAL TO DO.
WAIT... THERE'S ONE THING!

AND WHAT'S THAT?
STARTING IN FOURTH GRADE, WE HAVE TO TAKE TURNS CLEANING THE EXHIBIT ROOM.
WHAT ABOUT THE LOWER-GRADE ZEROES?
THEY PROBABLY WANDERED IN THERE WHEN IT USED TO BE KEPT OPEN. YOU KNOW, THAT ROOM IS PRETTY CREEPY; I'M NOT SURPRISED THAT SHADOWS GET LOST IN THERE!
WHAT'S WITH THE EXHIBIT ROOM?
A WHILE BACK THEY FOUND AN ANCIENT KILN BEHIND THE SCHOOL. THEY TOOK THE ARTIFACTS AND PUT THEM ON DISPLAY. THE SCHOOL CALLS IT AN EXHIBIT ROOM.
...BUT IT'S BASICALLY STORAGE FOR OLD POTS.
SO...THE SHADOWS DISAPPEARED IN THE EXHIBIT ROOM?!

WE'RE GOING TO INVESTIGATE THE EXHIBIT ROOM TOMORROW.
BUT FIRST...
...I NEED TO CHECK SOMETHING.
DID YOU COME HERE AGAIN BECAUSE NO ONE ELSE IS AROUND?
OBVIOUSLY.
WHY DON'T YOU SHOW ME TO PEOPLE ALREADY?
YOU KNOW, A LITTLE EARLIER, I THOUGHT I MIGHT, BUT I CHANGED MY MIND.
YOU'RE STAYING HIDDEN FOR THE TIME BEING.
WHY?
SOMETHING FISHY IS GOING ON.

WHAT IS IT?
THERE ARE THESE KIDS CALLED ZEROES AT SCHOOL, AND FOR SOME REASON THEY DON'T HAVE SHADOWS.
WHAT DOES THAT HAVE TO DO WITH ANYTHING?
THOSE KIDS LOOK LIKE THEY'VE TOTALLY LOST IT.
I THINK WHEN THEY LOSE THEIR SHADOWS, THEY LOSE SOMETHING IMPORTANT WITH IT.
BUT DO YOU KNOW WHERE THOSE ZEROES LOST THEIR SHADOWS?
THE EXHIBIT ROOM!
WHERE I FIRST MET *YOU!*

STORE
FRESH
WHAT WAS I EXPECTING?
SHE SAYS SHE ONLY REMEMBERS BEING IN A DARK PLACE...
AND SHE CAN'T TELL IF IT WAS THE EXHIBIT ROOM OR NOT.
I'M NOT SURE I BELIEVE HER, THOUGH. JUST CAUSE I DON'T REMEMBER WHAT HAPPENED, DOESN'T MEAN SHE DOESN'T!
SUPPLIES
BEST TO AVOID...
GOTCHA! CAREFUL... CAREFUL!
THIS TIME FOR SURE...

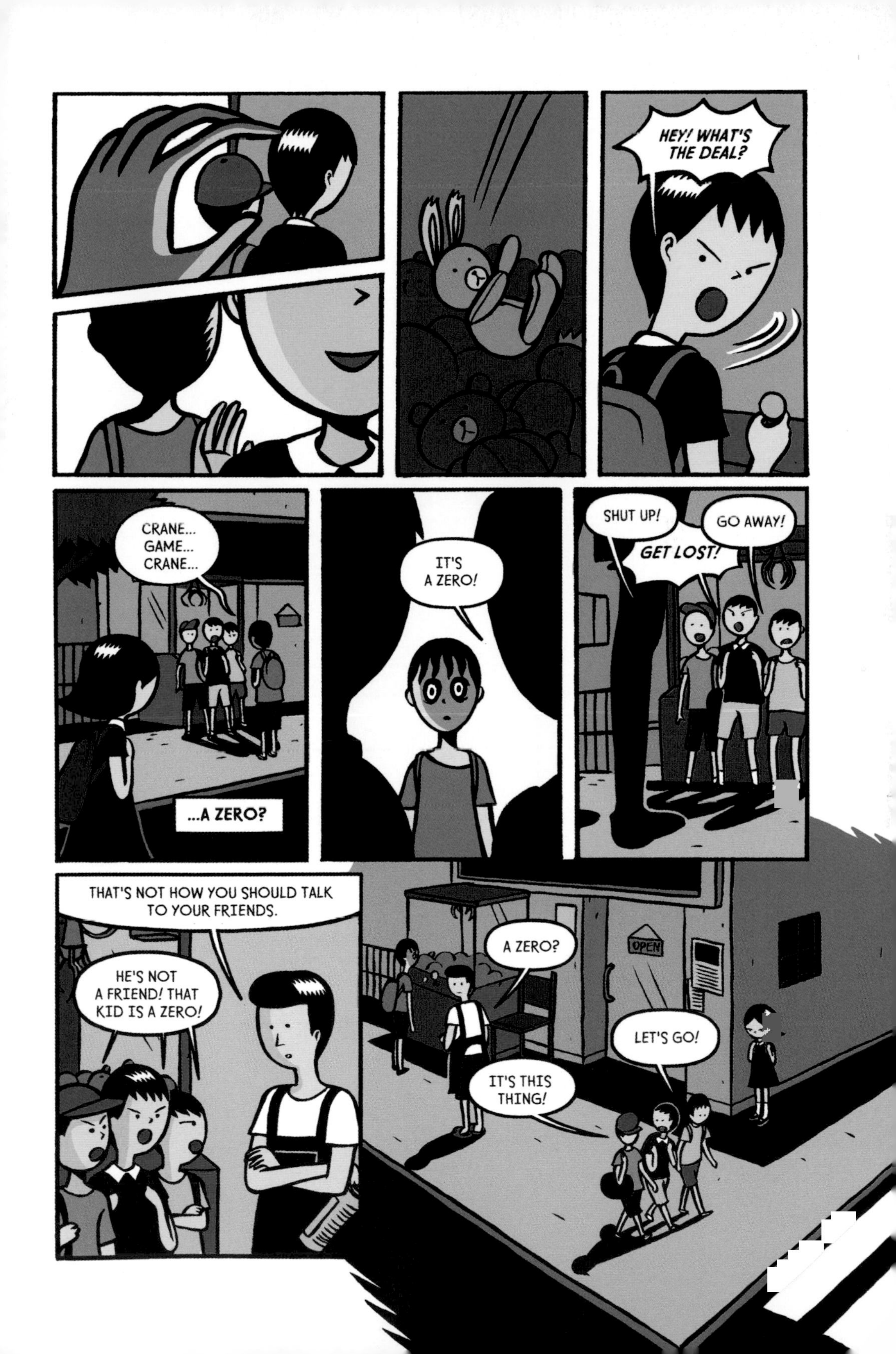
HEY! WHAT'S THE DEAL?
CRANE... GAME... CRANE...
...A ZERO?
IT'S A ZERO!
SHUT UP!
GO AWAY!
GET LOST!
THAT'S NOT HOW YOU SHOULD TALK TO YOUR FRIENDS.
HE'S NOT A FRIEND! THAT KID IS A ZERO!
A ZERO?
IT'S THIS THING!
LET'S GO!
OPEN

WHAT'S A ZERO?
SUPPLIES
PEN
DO YOU WANT TO TRY? I CAN HELP YOU.
WANT... TOY...
JUST PUT MONEY IN HERE, AND...
THAT MAN...HE CAN'T TELL THE DIFFERENCE?

7.
IN SHADOWS
WORK ALL DAY...IT NEVER STOPS.

NOT JUST THE GUY AT THE CORNER STORE, BUT NO ADULTS CAN SEE THE ZEROES.
ZEROES HAVE HOLLOW EYES AND NO SHADOWS, BUT ADULTS AREN'T ABLE TO NOTICE. TO THEM, IT JUST LOOKS LIKE THE KIDS ARE A LITTLE GLOOMY, THAT'S ALL.
THAT'S WHY NONE OF THE TEACHERS SEEM TO CARE THAT KIDS ARE LOSING THEIR SHADOWS.
OK, BUT HOW ON EARTH DO THESE KIDS LOSE THEIR SHADOWS?
YOU REALLY CAN'T REMEMBER A SINGLE THING THAT HAPPENED THAT DAY IN THE EXHIBIT ROOM?
I TOLD YOU, ALL I REMEMBER IS THAT IT WAS DARK.
HOW IS THAT POSSIBLE? DO YOU EVEN KNOW WHO YOU ARE?
OF COURSE! I'M YOUR SHADOW!

MAYBE MY SHADOW LOST HER MEMORIES ON THE SAME DAY THAT I LOST MY MEMORIES IN THE EXHIBIT ROOM.
STILL, IT'S TOO MUCH OF A COINCIDENCE THAT THE EXHIBIT ROOM IS WHERE ZEROES LOSE THEIR SHADOWS! DID MY SHADOW COME FROM SOMEONE ELSE?!
I HAVE TO REMEMBER WHAT HAPPENED THAT DAY!
WHAT ARE YOU SO WORRIED OVER?
HOW'D YOU GET BEHIND ME?
ISN'T IT COOL? I FEEL STRONGER THESE DAYS.

GET DOWN! YOU'RE NOT SUPPOSED TO BE THERE. THE LIGHT IS POINTING THE OTHER WAY!
IT DOESN'T MATTER WHERE IT'S POINTED. I CAN NOW BE ANYWHERE I WANT AS LONG AS THERE'S LIGHT NEARBY!
YOU'RE A SHADOW. ACT LIKE ONE!
ACT LIKE A SHADOW?
YOU SHOULD APPEAR OPPOSITE FROM WHERE THE LIGHT IS, MOVE THE WAY I MOVE, AND NOT TALK BACK LIKE YOU ALWAYS DO!
DON'T LOOK DOWN ON ME JUST BECAUSE I'M STUCK TO YOUR FEET!
I'M REMINDING YOU THAT YOU'RE JUST A SHADOW.
SO ACT LIKE ONE!
OR ELSE I'LL SEND YOU BACK TO THE DARK PLACE WHERE YOU CAME FROM!

ACT LIKE
A SHADOW?
SEND
ME BACK?
I'LL NEVER
LET YOU DO SUCH
A THING!

I FEEL WEIRD...
SOMETHING'S OFF...
PERFECT TIMING!
WHISK
LET'S EAT BREAKFAST TOGETHER, FOR OLD TIME'S SAKE...
GUESS I'LL HAVE TO EAT ALONE.

MY HEAD FEELS CLOUDY...
BAP
OWW!
WHAT'S EVERYONE LOOKING AT?

SOMETHING'S WRONG WITH ME...
WHAT'S GOING ON WITH MY FACE?
I HAVE NO EXPRESSION... JUST LIKE...A ZERO!
WHAT DO YOU THINK?

HOW ARE YOU HERE? IT'S TOO DARK INSIDE THE SCHOOL BUILDING FOR YOU!
BUT THE SUNLIGHT IS PRETTY STRONG HERE!
I DON'T USE THIS STAIRWAY BECAUSE IT'S TOO BRIGHT IN THE MORNINGS. HOW DID I END UP HERE?
THIS IS ALL BECAUSE OF WHAT YOU SAID LAST NIGHT.
WHAT I SAID?
IF YOU HADN'T SAID THAT STUFF ABOUT SENDING ME BACK, I WOULDN'T HAVE GONE THIS FAR!
WHAT THE HECK DID YOU DO?
I DON'T KNOW...

WHAT'S GOING ON? SOMETHING'S WRONG— VERY WRONG!
NOW YOU FEEL IT?
FEEL WHAT? WHAT ARE YOU TALKING ABOUT?
YOU'LL FIND OUT SOON ENOUGH!
I DON'T KNOW WHAT YOU'RE PLANNING, BUT YOU'D BETTER STOP IT RIGHT NOW!
UH...
I'LL SHOW YOU WHAT HAPPENS WHEN YOU TREAT ME UNFAIRLY!
TELL ME RIGHT NOW WHAT YOU'RE DOING!
SUEE?

YEJIN! AT THE WORST MOMENT POSSIBLE!
LOOK AT YOU. EXTRA GLOOMY TODAY.
SOMEONE KILL YOUR DOG?
EVEN WEIRDER THAN USUAL.
I NEED TO SAY SOMETHING TO SEND THEM AWAY!
WHAT ARE YOU STARING AT? CAT GOT YOUR TONGUE?
BUT...UGH...I CAN'T SPEAK!
WHY IS SHE POKING YEJIN'S SHADOW?
DON'T MOVE! THEY'LL NOTICE!
I NEED TO GET OUT OF HERE BEFORE THEY SEE SOMETHING!
BUT...
I CAN'T MOVE! I CAN'T MOVE ANYTHING!

LOOK AT HER FACE! SHE'S A TOTAL ZOMBIE!
WOOSH WOOSH
WHAT IS SHE DOING?
STOP!
YOU THINK SHE'S A ZERO NOW?
REALLY? SUEE LEE, A ZERO?
I'M A ZERO?
SEOYEON, ARE YOU STUPID?
HUH?
LOOK AT HER EYES. THOSE AREN'T ZERO EYES!
I... GUESS?

SEOYEON'S SHADOW! IT'S PUSHED IN!
WHAT...IS SHE DOING?
LET'S GET OUT OF HERE!
SUEE WILL END UP IN ZERO CLASS ANYWAY. I TOLD MY MOM TO SEND HER THERE!
PHEW, THAT WAS CLOSE. GOOD THING THEY DIDN'T NOTICE!
BUT...WHAT WAS THAT ALL ABOUT?

SEOYEON'S SHADOW...
IT WAS LIKE HAEUN'S.
WHEN MY SHADOW POKED IT,
IT WAS SOFT LIKE RUBBER.
BUT YEJIN'S SHADOW WAS AS HARD AS ROCK. MY SHADOW POKED IT, BUT IT DIDN'T BUDGE.
WHY?
WHAT MAKES THEM DIFFERENT?
SUEE!
WHAT'S WRONG WITH YOU?

YOUR FACE IS DARK AND GLOOMY. IS SOMETHING WRONG?
NOT LIKE YOU CARE.
WAIT...DID I JUST SAY THAT?
OK, I GET IT. YOU'RE IN A BAD MOOD.
SHE'S POKING AGAIN!
HYUNWOO'S SHADOW IS SOLID!
I FIGURED OUT WHERE WE CAN LEARN MORE ABOUT THE EXHIBIT ROOM. GONNA CHECK IT OUT LATER. WHAT DO YOU THINK?
WHATEVER.
WHERE ARE THESE WORDS COMING FROM?

WE MIGHT FIND SOME IMPORTANT CLUES. YOU'RE REALLY NOT INTERESTED?
I DON'T CARE.
THESE...AREN'T MY WORDS!
ARE YOU SICK OR SOMETHING?
NO MORE INVESTIGATING.
THEN WHOSE WORDS ARE THEY?
WHAT DO YOU MEAN BY THAT?
SOMETHING IS TERRIBLY WRONG!
HOW DOES SUEE LEE KNOW HYUNWOO?!
GET LOST!

DID...YOU JUST TELL ME... TO GET LOST?
NO! THAT'S NOT ME SPEAKING!
I HAVE TO TELL HIM... BUT MY LIPS AREN'T MOVING!
I'M TRAPPED WITHIN MY BODY!
WHAT'S WRONG WITH YOU?
I DON'T KNOW WHAT'S WRONG!
THIS ISN'T ME!
FINE, THEN I'LL GET LOST.
WHO WAS THAT?
WHAT ARE THOSE TWO TALKING ABOUT?

I CAN'T CONTROL MY WORDS OR MY ACTIONS!
EVER SINCE I WOKE UP...
I'VE FELT LIKE I'M NOT MYSELF.
MY SHADOW HAD BEEN THREATENING ME EARLIER... SAYING THINGS ABOUT "GOING THIS FAR," BLAMING ME...
IS MY SHADOW...
...CONTROLLING ME?
IT'S TOO DARK HERE! I WANT TO LEAVE!
EVERYTHING I SAID AND DID, THAT WAS MY SHADOW?
WHAT'S GOING ON? I FEEL SO HELPLESS!

SUEE, DO YOU HAVE TIME FOR A CHAT?
SO, LAST SEMESTER, EVERY STUDENT TOOK SOMETHING CALLED A DEVELOPMENT EXAM.
BUT SINCE YOU JUST TRANSFERRED, YOU DIDN'T TAKE THE TEST.
I WANTED TO LET YOU KNOW THAT THE SCHOOL HAS DECIDED...
THAT YOU WILL ALSO BE TAKING THE EXAM ON AN UPCOMING...
SHE'S JUST WALKING AWAY? TSK-TSK.
WHERE ARE WE GOING? ANSWER ME!
WHERE ARE YOU TAKING ME?

ARE WE BEHIND THE SCHOOL?
DIDN'T I SAY TO BRING FIVE DOLLARS TODAY?
MOM WENT TO WORK EARLY. I COULDN'T GET THE MONEY!
WHY ARE WE GOING TO THOSE KIDS?
YOU THINK THAT'S AN EXCUSE?
I'LL... I'LL BRING IT TOMORROW! I PROMISE! GIVE ME ONE MORE CHANCE!
THAT'S WHAT YOU SAID YESTERDAY! YOU FORGOT ALREADY?
VICE PRINCIPAL SAYS YOU GUYS ARE TOO LOUD.
WHO ARE YOU?
WHAT ARE YOU DOING?!

HE SAID HE'LL COME GET YOU GUYS IF YOU DON'T SHUT UP.
WHAT?!
LOOK AT HER— SHE'S COMPLETELY SERIOUS!
I THINK IT'S REAL!
OK, WE'RE GOOD FOR TODAY!
FOOSH
MY SHADOW JUST HELPED THAT KID!
BUT WHY?

I'LL BE YOUR FRIEND.
WAIT...THOSE WORDS...!
REALLY?
THAT'S WHAT THE SHADOW SAID TO ME BEFORE I PASSED OUT IN THE EXHIBIT ROOM!
WHOA... WHAT'S THAT?
YOUR SHADOW IS MOVING!
WHAT ARE YOU DOING?
I SAID, WHAT ARE YOU DOING?!

SOMETHING VERY
WRONG IS HAPPENING!
HEY, KID, RUN
AWAY! NOW!
IT WILL BE FUN...

8. FRIEND

SUEE... SAID THAT...?
AT FIRST I THOUGHT IT WAS 'CAUSE SHE WAS SICK...
...BUT SOMETHING ABOUT IT FELT STRANGE. LIKE, I WAS DEFINITELY TALKING TO SUEE, BUT IT DIDN'T FEEL LIKE HER. DID ANYTHING SEEM OFF TO YOU?
YEAH... A LITTLE BIT...
IT'S HER...

WHISK
LOOK AT HER. DEFINITELY WEIRD! LIKE SHE'S...
...A ZERO!
BUT...
I KNOW. SHE HAS A SHADOW!
SO, WHY DOES IT KEEP FEELING LIKE SHE'S A ZERO?

NO WAY!
HOW COULD YOU DO SUCH A THING?
YOU DIDN'T KNOW?
I HAD NO IDEA!
HOW COULD YOU NOT KNOW?
I THOUGHT WE FOUND...
...THAT ZEROES WERE MADE IN THE EXHIBIT ROOM!

BUT YOU...HOW DID YOU?
THIS ISN'T THE FIRST TIME, IS IT?
YOU WERE POKING EVERYONE'S SHADOWS...
TO CHOOSE THE ONES YOU LIKED!
I LIKE PEOPLE LIKE HER. LIKE HAEUN.
FOR HOW LONG? SINCE WHEN?
DON'T PLAY DUMB!

P-PLAY DUMB?
COME ON, YOU KNOW IT'S BEEN HAPPENING RIGHT FROM THE BEGINNING!
DRAT, WHY DO THEY KEEP PUSHING?!
THINK CAREFULLY!
IT'S NOT MY FAULT!
I CAN APPEAR ONLY WHEN YOU'RE ANNOYED!
AND I'M ALWAYS STUCK TO YOUR FEET!
I CAN ONLY GO WHERE YOU GO...
I'M YOUR SHADOW!

BUT...I...DIDN'T KNOW! I HAD NO IDEA!
NO!
YOU JUST PRETENDED NOT TO KNOW!
THE SAME WAY YOU IGNORED...
...HAEUN,
AND THE OTHER KIDS WHO ARE BULLIED.

NO...IT'S NOT THE SAME!
I JUST DON'T LIKE GETTING INVOLVED IN OTHER PEOPLE'S BUSINESS!
THAT'S NOT THE SAME AS IGNORING PEOPLE!
FROM THE OTHER SIDE, IT'S ALL THE SAME. I KNEW IT. YOU ONLY THINK ABOUT YOURSELF. YOU DON'T CARE ABOUT ANYONE ELSE!
WHAT GIVES YOU THE RIGHT TO SAY THAT? I SAW WHAT YOU DID TO THAT KID!
HE WAS LONELY.

I COULD
TELL WHEN I TOUCHED
HIS SHADOW.
I WAS
JUST DOING WHAT HE
WANTED.
I BECAME
HIS FRIEND!
IS THAT HOW YOU
MAKE FRIENDS?
BY TURNING HIM INTO
A ZERO?!

I DON'T KNOW ABOUT THAT—I JUST BECAME HIS FRIEND!
YOU STOLE HIS SHADOW!
NO! I BECAME HIS FRIEND!
WHAT KIND OF NONSENSE IS THAT?
WHAT DO YOU KNOW ABOUT FRIENDS? YOU DON'T HAVE A SINGLE ONE! YOU'RE A LONER!
NO, I HAVE FRIENDS!
SUEE...
WHAT ARE YOU DOING HERE?

MEANWHILE...
OUTSKIRTS DAILY
HISTORY OF OUTSKIRTS ELEMENTARY
THIS IS FROM SIX YEARS AGO, WHEN THE EXHIBIT ROOM WAS UNVEILED!
WHY ARE YEJIN'S PARENTS IN THE PICTURE?

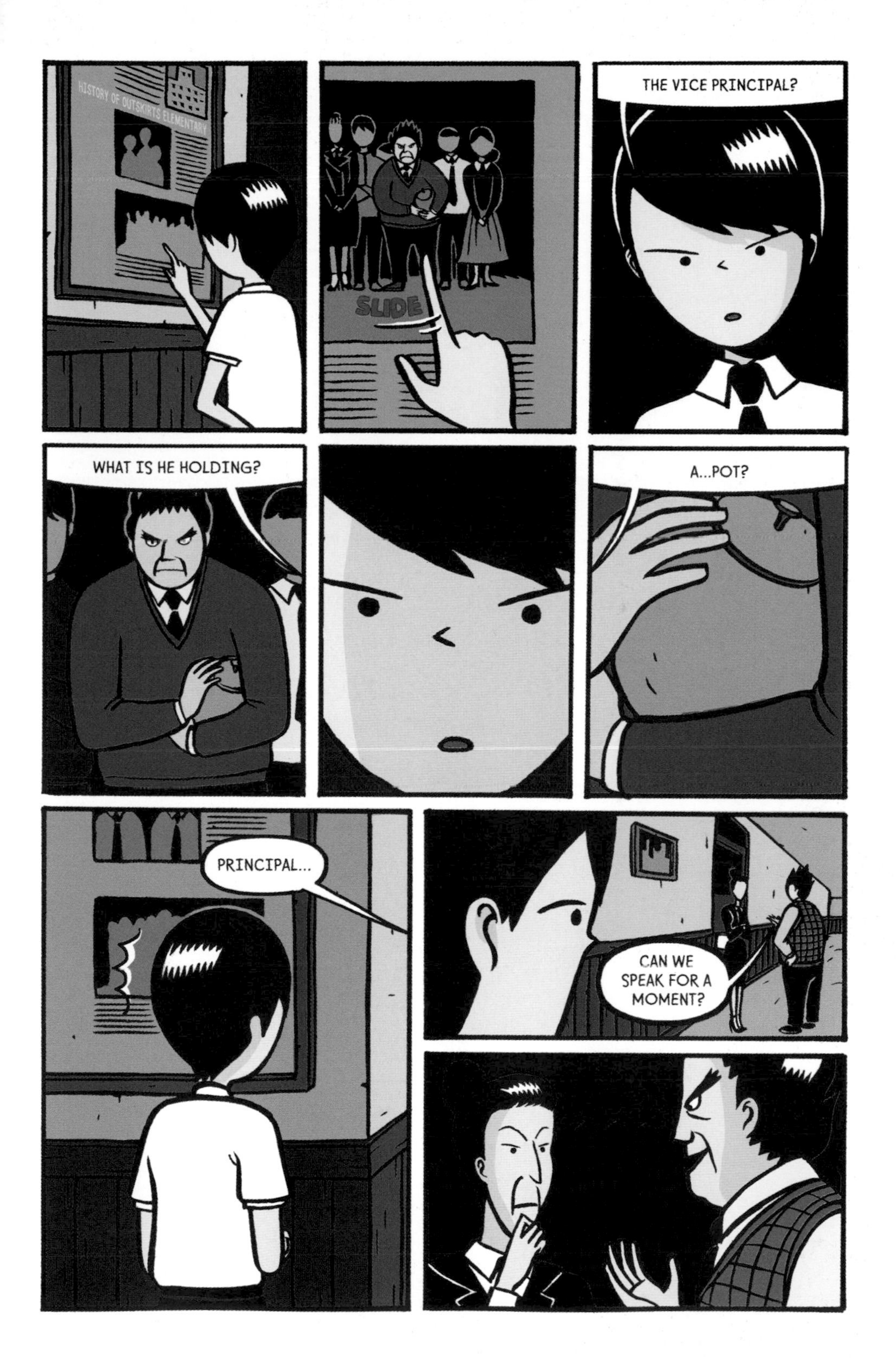
HISTORY OF OUTSKIRTS ELEMENTARY
SLIDE
THE VICE PRINCIPAL?
WHAT IS HE HOLDING?
A...POT?
PRINCIPAL...
CAN WE SPEAK FOR A MOMENT?

IT WILL BE VERY GOOD FOR THE SCHOOL'S FUTURE, IS WHAT I'M SAYING.
IS THAT SO?
YES. WE NEED TO HAVE MORE AFTER-SCHOOL CLASSES.
IT SEEMS YOU HAVE ALREADY MADE PLANS.
OF COURSE. YOU KNOW ME TOO WELL.
WHISPER WHISPER

HAEUN...
I THOUGHT... YOU MIGHT BE HERE...
YOU...
THE WAY YOU ARE...
IS IT... BECAUSE OF THE SHADOW?
WHY DON'T YOU COME CLOSER?
NO!
NOT HAEUN!

COME HERE.
I'LL SHOW YOU.
HAEUN! DON'T COME!
IS THAT... OK?
A LITTLE CLOSER.
HAEUN! NO! DON'T COME NEAR ME!
YOUR SHADOW...WHAT IS IT DOING?
SHE JUST...
...WANTS TO BE FRIENDS.

WHAT ARE YOU HIDING?
OH, RIGHT...
THIS...
IT'S ZERO DETECTIVE CLUB DOLLS...
I WAS REALLY HAPPY... TO BE PART OF THE CLUB...
SO...I MADE THEM... I HOPE YOU... LIKE THEM..

I GUESS...
YOU DON'T...
HAEUN...
SORRY...
I'M NOT VERY
GOOD AT IT...
SNAP
NO!!!

SUEE...
SORRY...

HAEUN...
STUMBLE
HUH...?!
HAEUN IS...
WHAT'S...
HAPPENING?
THUD
...A ZERO...
BECAUSE OF ME!

SUEE...
SORRY...
NO...
NO...
NO...
HAEUN...

I'M...SORRY...

9.
TOGETHER
HAIR SALO
CLANG
REALTY
REALTY

SQUEAK
HI, MR. CHOI!
OH, LOOK WHO'S HERE.
GRAMPS, GRANDMA SAYS DINNER'S READY.
HMM...
HAVE YOU EATEN, HYUNWOO?
I HAVE. HOW LONG DO YOU THINK IT WILL TAKE?
IT MAY TAKE A WHILE. COME SIT OVER HERE WHILE YOU WAIT.
OK.
HAVE YOU HEARD YOUR SCHOOL'S CLOSING DOWN THE EXHIBIT ROOM?
NO. WHAT'S GOING ON?

YOU KNOW SOMETHING ABOUT THE EXHIBIT ROOM, DON'T YOU?
SURE I DO.
COULD YOU TELL ME A LITTLE ABOUT IT?
ABOUT THE EXHIBIT ROOM, YOU SAY? WHERE DO I BEGIN...
YOU KNOW THERE'S AN OLD KILN IN THE MOUNTAINS, RIGHT?
YES, I HEARD THAT'S WHERE THEY FOUND THE POTS IN THE EXHIBIT ROOM.
YOU'RE NOT TELLING THAT LUDICROUS STORY AGAIN, ARE YOU?
AHEM... BEAR WITH ME FOR THIS ONE.
THERE'S AN URBAN LEGEND ABOUT THE KILN.
AN URBAN LEGEND?

THERE ONCE LIVED A SKILLED POTTER IN OUR VILLAGE.
SINCE HIS WIFE'S DEATH, HE'D BEEN LIVING WITH HIS YOUNG DAUGHTER.
ONE DAY, A CLOAKED FIGURE APPEARED.
THIS CLIENT GAVE THE POTTER A BAGFUL OF MYSTERIOUS POWDER, PROMISING HIM A HANDSOME REWARD IF HE COULD MAKE A SMALL POT. BUT THE CLIENT WARNED THE POTTER NEVER TO OPEN IT.
THE POTTER PUT HIS EVERYTHING INTO THE WORK, BUT THE POWDER WASN'T IDEAL FOR CRAFTING A POT. HE DIDN'T GIVE UP, THOUGH; HE KEPT WATCH ON THE FIRE AND EVENTUALLY MADE IT WORK.
A FEW DAYS LATER, THE CLIENT CAME TO THE KILN TO PICK UP THE POT, BUT IT WAS EMPTY.
THE POTTER AND HIS DAUGHTER HAD MYSTERIOUSLY DISAPPEARED.
BUT WHY WOULD THEY DISAPPEAR?
RUMOR HAS IT THAT THE POT WAS CURSED AND HAD TAKEN AWAY THE DAUGHTER'S SOUL.

SADDENED, THE POTTER REALIZED THE POT WAS CURSED. HE DECIDED TO HIDE THE POT SO THE CURSE COULD NEVER HARM ANYONE AGAIN.
HE SPENT THE REST OF HIS LIFE SEARCHING FOR HIS DAUGHTER'S SOUL.
BUT WHAT'S IT GOT TO DO WITH THE EXHIBIT ROOM?
WELL, THEY FOUND THE KILN AT THE CONSTRUCTION SITE WHEN THEY WERE BUILDING YOUR SCHOOL.
THEN THEY DECIDED TO CHANGE THE PLAN AND MOVE AWAY FROM THERE.
AND WHEN THEY RESUMED THE CONSTRUCTION WHERE YOUR SCHOOL'S LOCATED TODAY, THEY DISCOVERED A DUMP AND A PILE OF SHATTERED POTS IN THERE...
AND, ULTIMATELY, THE POT FROM THE LEGEND, PERFECTLY PRESERVED, FLAWLESS, WITHOUT A SINGLE SCRATCH.
REALLY?
IT'S JUST A RUBBISH OLD TALE. ALL MADE UP.
BUT IT GOT THEM ALL THE DONATIONS THEY NEEDED TO BUILD THE EXHIBIT ROOM.
HOW DO YOU KNOW THAT'S THE POT FROM THE LEGEND? WHAT EVIDENCE DO WE HAVE?
NO ONE HAS EVER MANAGED TO OPEN IT. THERE'S DEFINITELY SOMETHING ABOUT THAT POT!
WHAT MORE DO WE NEED?
IF YOU SAY SO...
NOW... HOW SHOULD I MAKE MY NEXT MOVE?

HAIR SALON
WHAT A STORY! I CAN'T WAIT TO TELL SUEE!
HAS SHE ALREADY GONE TO BED? SHE DIDN'T LOOK SO WELL TODAY...
GET LOST!
WHY BOTHER? SHE TOLD ME TO GET LOST!
HAIR SALON
OPEN
BUT...THIS IS PRETTY IMPORTANT. I HAVE TO FIND HER!

BUZZ-
BUZZ-
QUIET...
OUTSKIRTS CLEANERS
OPEN
DON'T WORRY, THEY CAN'T HAVE GONE TOO FAR. I'LL GO LOOK FOR THEM!
WHERE COULD THEY HAVE GONE?
OUTSKIRTS CLEANERS

BLARE
WHAT DO I DO NOW?
HAEUN...
I'M SO, SO SORRY...
LIES! YOU ARE NOT!

HOW DID IT COME TO THIS? WHY DID IT HAVE TO BE MY SHADOW?
ISN'T THAT OBVIOUS? BECAUSE YOU'RE THE MEAN ONE. YOU ALWAYS HAVE BEEN.
WHAT? YOU ARE THE ONE WHO WON'T LEAVE ME ALONE!
WHATEVER!
CLENCH
GET OUT OF MY HEAD!
IT DOESN'T CHANGE ANYTHING, SILLY!
...GET OUT!

YOU CAN'T GET ME OUT OF YOUR HEAD!
WHOOSH
YES, I CAN! AND I WILL!
I'M YOUR SHADOW! YOU CAN NEVER GET RID OF ME!
NO, IT DOESN'T WORK THAT WAY. YOU'RE MY SHADOW, AND I AM THE ONE IN CHARGE!
YOU LISTEN TO ME! NOW!
NOT A CHANCE!
WHOOSH-
HERE YOU ARE!
SWISH
WHAT ARE YOU GUYS DOING HERE?

HAEUN, YOUR PARENTS ARE WORRIED SICK ABOUT YOU.
WAIT...YOU GUYS...
WHAT'S HAPPENED? HAEUN! LOOK AT ME!
YOU SAID YOU WERE GOING HOME! HOW DID YOU BECOME A ZERO?
NO...
SUEE! WHEN DID SHE BECOME LIKE THIS? WHEN?
COME CLOSER. I'LL TELL YOU.
SUEE...

WHAT'S... THAT?! YOUR SHADOW...IT'S MOVING!
COME ON, IT'LL BE FUN.
NO, NOT HYUNWOO'S SHADOW! LEAVE IT ALONE!
GRIN
HYUNWOO! RUN! RUN!
POKE
NOOOO!
HIS SHADOW...

...SUCKS! I DON'T LIKE HIM!
WHAT THE? IT TALKS!
PHEW, JUST LIKE I THOUGHT! SHE CAN ONLY STEAL FROM BULLIED KIDS!
WHAT IS IT TRYING TO DO?
HMMFF! HMMMFFF!
STOP TUGGING AT HIS SHADOW! HE'S POPULAR AT SCHOOL. WHATEVER YOU DO, IT DOESN'T WORK!
IF YOU KEEP DOING THAT... STOOOOP, IT'S ANNOYING!
HMMF! HMMMFF!!
STOP...I SAID...STOP!!
SUEE! JUST WHAT IN THE WORLD IS YOUR SHADOW UP TO? AND WHAT'S GOING ON WITH YOU?
YEAH...WHAT'S REALLY GOING ON WITH ME?

MY SHADOW SHOWS UP WHENEVER I'M UPSET...
IT'S SO ANNOYING!
BUT AT SOME POINT SHE STARTED MAKING ME ANGRY WHENEVER SHE SHOWED UP.
I THINK...SHE'S FEEDING ON MY ANGER!
THAT'S WHY SHE WANTS ME TO BE SO ANGRY ALL THE TIME!
I HAVE TO GET THROUGH THIS. I WILL GET THROUGH THIS! FOR HAEUN! BUT...HOW?
SHE'S ONLY GETTING STRONGER AND STRONGER!
WHAT IF...I STAY CALM?
WHAT ARE YOU UP TO THIS TIME?

I CAN STOP THIS.
TILT
NO! NO! NO!
TREMBLE TREMBLE
NO! NO! NO!
GRAB
HYUNWOO, I'VE DONE IT! I'VE GOT MY VOICE BACK!
YOUR VOICE? WHAT ARE YOU TALKING ABOUT?
I TOLD HIM EVERYTHING—MY SHADOW, HAEUN...

WHY ARE YOU TELLING ME THIS NOW?
I HAD NO IDEA THIS WOULD HAPPEN.
AND I THOUGHT I COULD HANDLE IT ON MY OWN.
NO...
YOU DIDN'T TRUST US AS YOUR FRIENDS, AND YOU STILL DON'T.
DOPP-
DOPP-

NOOO, I HATE RAIN!
URGH...
CLEANERS
OUTSKIRTS CLEANERS
OPEN

YOU LIVE IN THE SALON?
MY GRANDMA RUNS THE HAIR SALON ON THE FIRST FLOOR AND WE LIVE UPSTAIRS.
HYUNWOO LIVES NEXT DOOR?
DID YOU ALREADY KNOW I LIVE IN THE BETWEEN HOUSE?
WHO DOESN'T?
HOW COME I HAVEN'T SEEN YOU AROUND?
I DUNNO. PROBABLY YOU DIDN'T CARE.
I DIDN'T...
CARE...?

...HYUNWOO WAS ALWAYS SO NICE TO ME...
ALWAYS THERE TO HELP...
BUT I NEVER RETURNED THE FAVOR. NEVER SAID THANK YOU.
OPEN
I'VE...I'VE DONE THAT BEFORE AS WELL.
OPEN
TURNING IN A BLANK ANSWER SHEET. I'VE DONE IT ONCE.
WE WERE TAKING A SPELLING TEST BACK IN THE FIRST GRADE, AND I JUST TURNED IN A BLANK PIECE OF PAPER.
OPEN
SO HOW DID THAT GO?

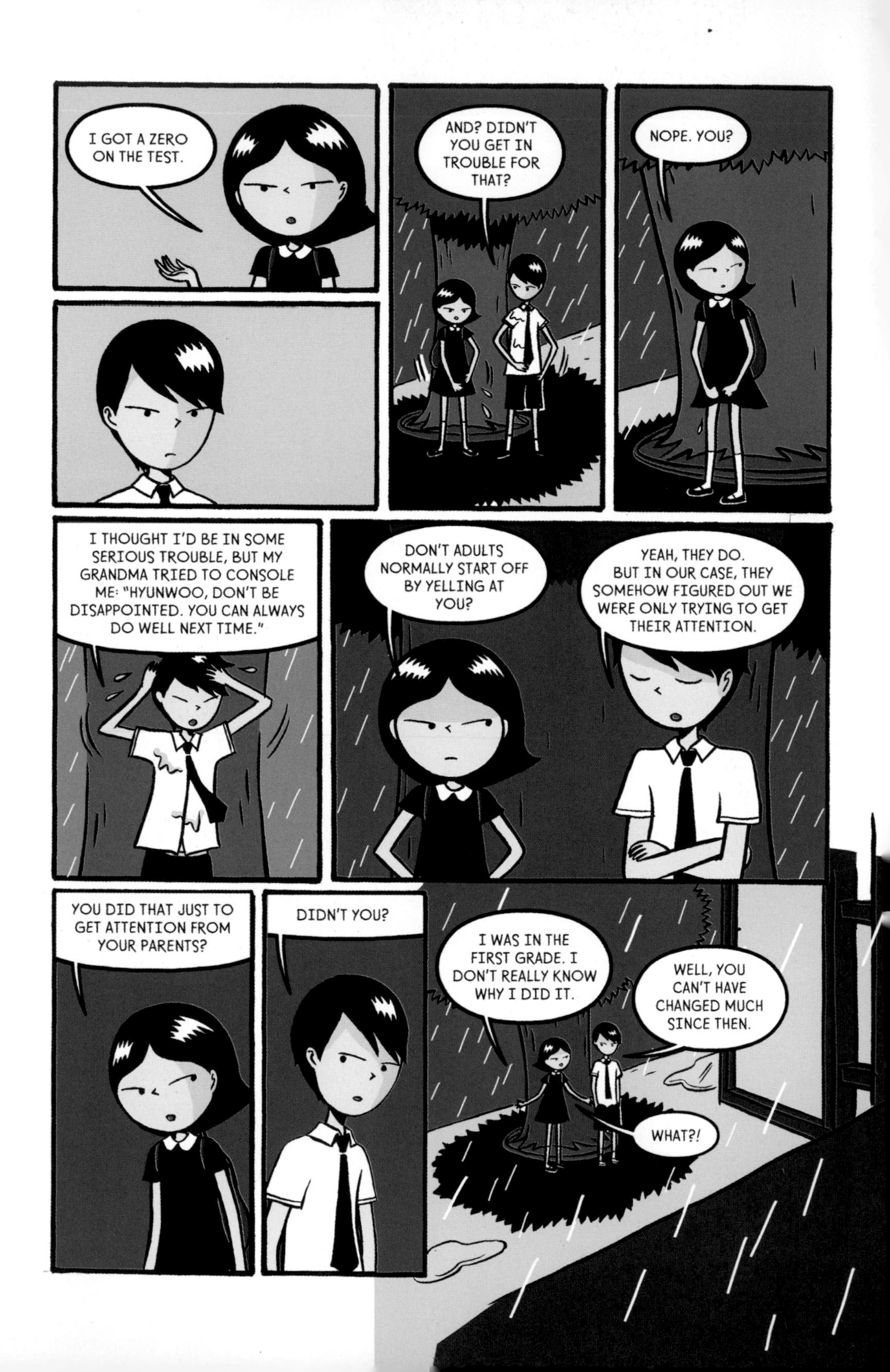
I GOT A ZERO ON THE TEST.
AND? DIDN'T YOU GET IN TROUBLE FOR THAT?
NOPE. YOU?
I THOUGHT I'D BE IN SOME SERIOUS TROUBLE, BUT MY GRANDMA TRIED TO CONSOLE ME: "HYUNWOO, DON'T BE DISAPPOINTED. YOU CAN ALWAYS DO WELL NEXT TIME."
DON'T ADULTS NORMALLY START OFF BY YELLING AT YOU?
YEAH, THEY DO. BUT IN OUR CASE, THEY SOMEHOW FIGURED OUT WE WERE ONLY TRYING TO GET THEIR ATTENTION.
YOU DID THAT JUST TO GET ATTENTION FROM YOUR PARENTS?
DIDN'T YOU?
I WAS IN THE FIRST GRADE. I DON'T REALLY KNOW WHY I DID IT.
WELL, YOU CAN'T HAVE CHANGED MUCH SINCE THEN.
WHAT?!

MY PARENTS GOT DIVORCED WHEN I WAS FIVE, AND I HAVEN'T SEEN MY MOM SINCE THEN.
SO WHEN MY TEACHER WAS READING US A WORD, IT SOMEHOW REMINDED ME OF MY MOM.
SPELL "DELICIOUS."
I DIDN'T WANT TO WRITE ANYTHING DOWN.
SO I TURNED IN THE BLANK SHEET.
HAVE YOU SEEN HER SINCE?
SHE LIVES SOMEWHERE FAR AWAY FROM HERE. AND SHE VISITS ME ONCE IN A WHILE.
MY PARENTS LIVE FAR AWAY, TOO...IT'S NOT LIKE WHAT BYEONGTAE'S BEEN BABBLING ABOUT...IT'S COMPLICATED. I LIVE WITH MY GRANDPARENTS.
DON'T LET IT GET TO YOU. HE'S NOT WORTH IT. HE ONLY SEES WHATEVER HE CHOOSES TO SEE.
YOU'RE RIGHT! I SHOULD JUST IGNORE HIM, BUT IT'S DIFFICULT SOMETIMES.

ANYWAY, THAT'S NOT EXACTLY THE REASON I TURNED IN THE BLANK SHEET, THOUGH. I JUST WANTED TO KNOW WHAT IT'D FEEL LIKE TO GET A ZERO ON A TEST.
I WAS GETTING A BIT TIRED OF BEING THE TOP STUDENT.
SHOW-OFF.
I THINK IT'D BE BETTER IF I SKIPPED SCHOOL TOMORROW.
WHAT DO YOU MEAN?
I'M NOT SURE IF CAN CONTROL MY SHADOW.
IT'S SO NOT LIKE YOU.
AND WHAT ABOUT HAEUN? WHAT DO WE DO ABOUT HER SHADOW?
I... DON'T KNOW YET. BUT I WILL FIGURE IT OUT.
WE WILL! HAEUN'S OUR FRIEND. LET ME HELP YOU. WE WILL TRY TO FIGURE THINGS OUT TOMORROW AT SCHOOL. I'M SURE WE WILL COME UP WITH SOMETHING. TOGETHER.
TOGETHER?

10.
DILEMMA
I THINK I'VE CHANGED A LITTLE SINCE MY SHADOW CAME ALIVE.

I WAS USED TO TAKING THINGS INTO MY OWN HANDS. I WAS TRYING TO HANDLE IT ON MY OWN THIS TIME, TOO. I STARTED ALL THIS.
SO IT WAS A BIT OF A SURPRISE WHEN HYUNWOO OFFERED TO HELP.
BUT IT DOESN'T FEEL HALF AS BAD AS I THOUGHT. IT ACTUALLY FEELS NICE TO HAVE SOMEONE ON MY SIDE.
WHAT ARE YEJIN'S PARENTS DOING WITH THE VICE PRINCIPAL?
HMM... GOOD QUESTION.
MORNING, Y'ALL.
WHISK
GOOD MORNING!
THEY TOOK... SUEE...TO THE... NURSE...
SHE LOOKS A BIT PEAKY. IS SHE ALL RIGHT?
YOU DON'T LOOK WELL EITHER.
I'M FINE!
NO, NO, SUEE IS TOTALLY FINE.

WELL, IF YOU SAY SO. HAVE A GOOD DAY, YOU THREE.
IN FRONT OF THE MUSIC ROOM.
GAGGLE GAGGLE
WHAT'S GOING ON? YOU GUYS STAY HERE. I'LL BE RIGHT BACK.
WHAT?
NO WAY!
NOTICE:
ALL STUDENTS ARE REQUIRED TO TAKE AFTER-SCHOOL CLASS
DUE TO NEW REGULATIONS, ALL STUDENTS WILL BE REQUIRED TO TAKE AT LEAST ONE SEMESTER OF AFTER-SCHOOL CLASS IN ORDER TO GRADUATE. MORE DETAILS TO FOLLOW.
— VICE PRINCIPAL
EVERYONE HAS TO GO TO AFTER-SCHOOL CLASS?!
YEAH. I THINK IT'S ALL PART OF THE VICE PRINCIPAL'S SCHEME TO SORT OUT MORE ZEROS.
LOOK. HE MUST BE MAKING MORE SPACE FOR AFTER-SCHOOL CLASS.

MY DAD'S IN CHARGE OF THE MUSIC ROOM REMODELING.
WOW, IS HE REALLY?
YEAH. MY DAD'S IN CHARGE OF ALL THE CONSTRUCTION IN THE SCHOOL.
SINCE WHEN HAS YOUR DAD BEEN IN CHARGE?
SINCE MY FAMILY MOVED TO OUTSKIRTSVILLE. WHY?
OH, NOTHING. I WAS JUST CURIOUS...
SUEE LEE, WHY ARE *YOU* HERE? OH, LET ME GUESS. YOU'RE SO EXCITED TO BE IN THE ZERO CLASS, AREN'T YOU?
YOU LITTLE...!
TWITCH

GUYS, LOOK AT HAEUN. SHE'S A PERFECT ZERO WITH THAT EMPTY FACE!
SUEE, LET'S GO! I HAVE SOMETHING I NEED TO SHOW YOU!
WHY IS HE ALWAYS HANGING OUT WITH THOSE LOSERS?!
THIS PICTURE WAS TAKEN SIX YEARS AGO AT THE GROUNDBREAKING CEREMONY OF THE EXHIBIT ROOM.
WHEN I FIRST SAW THIS PICTURE, I WONDERED WHY YEJIN'S PARENTS WERE THERE AT THE CEREMONY.
PARTICIPANT IN TRADITION PRESERVATION--GROUNDBREAKING CEREMONY.
YEJIN JUST ANSWERED MY QUESTION.
AND ANOTHER THING IS...THIS.
A POT?

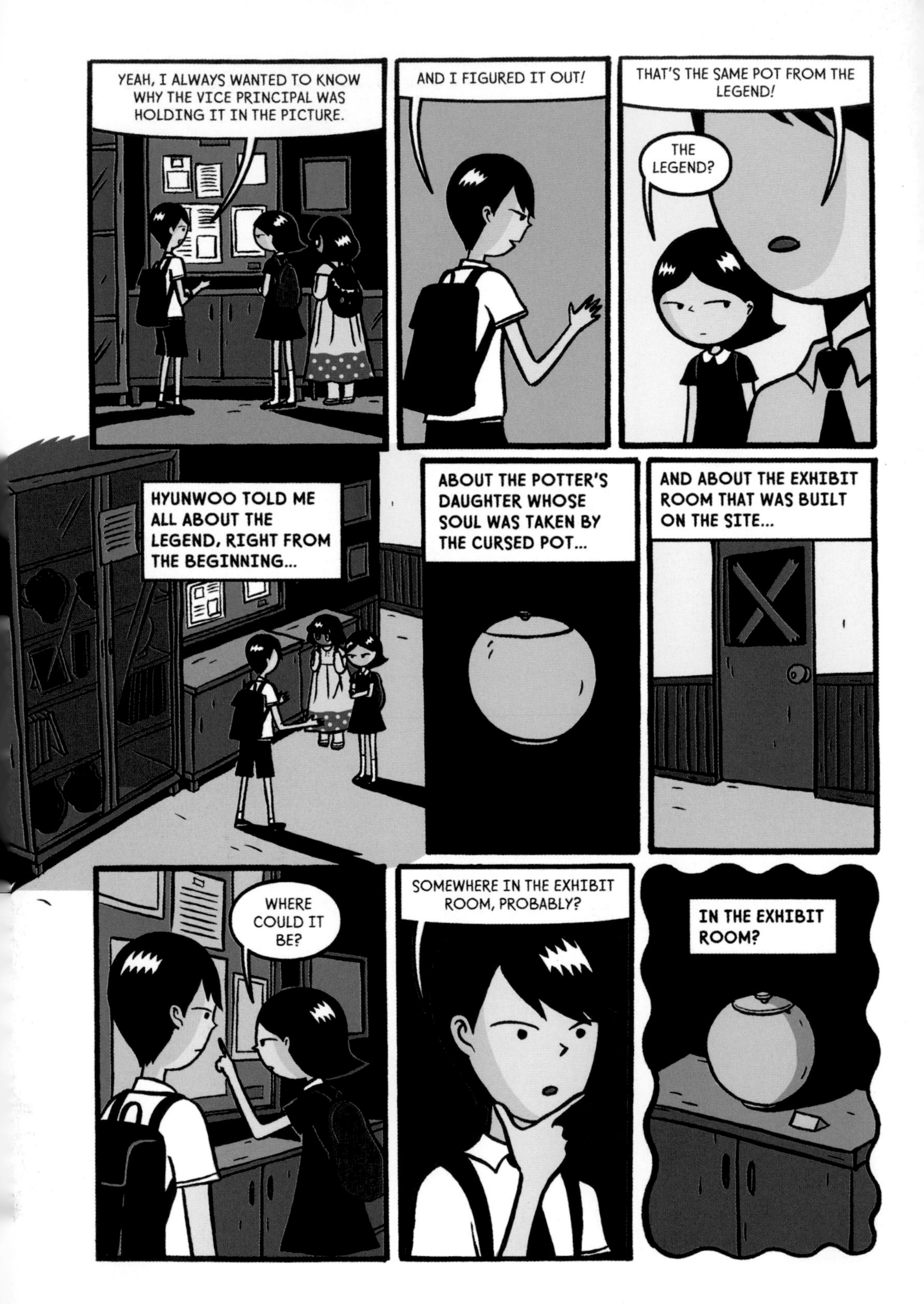
YEAH, I ALWAYS WANTED TO KNOW WHY THE VICE PRINCIPAL WAS HOLDING IT IN THE PICTURE.
AND I FIGURED IT OUT!
THAT'S THE SAME POT FROM THE LEGEND!
THE LEGEND?
HYUNWOO TOLD ME ALL ABOUT THE LEGEND, RIGHT FROM THE BEGINNING...
ABOUT THE POTTER'S DAUGHTER WHOSE SOUL WAS TAKEN BY THE CURSED POT...
AND ABOUT THE EXHIBIT ROOM THAT WAS BUILT ON THE SITE...
WHERE COULD IT BE?
SOMEWHERE IN THE EXHIBIT ROOM, PROBABLY?
IN THE EXHIBIT ROOM?

THE POT KINDA LOOKS FAMILIAR.
DOES IT?
THE EXHIBIT ROOM...THE POT... THE VOICE...
I DON'T HAVE A MOM EITHER!
THE VOICE FROM THE EXHIBIT ROOM SAID IT DIDN'T HAVE A MOM.
WHAT?
I WOULD'VE JUST WALKED AWAY IF I HADN'T HEARD IT.
COME HERE...LET'S TALK...
I FOLLOWED THE VOICE...AND THERE I SAW A POT!
THE VOICE WAS COMING FROM THE POT!
THEN IT MEANS...YOUR SHADOW IS...
MY SHADOW?
THAT... WE'LL HAVE TO ASK.
LET'S GO FIND THE POT!

EXHIBIT ROOM
CREEK
EXHIBIT ROOM
THERE'S NO ONE GUARDING THE EXHIBIT ROOM.
BUT WHERE DO WE FIND THE KEY TO THE EXHIBIT ROOM?
WE DON'T NEED A KEY.
WHAT DO YOU MEAN?
SOMEONE'S LEFT THE DOOR OPEN!
WICKED!
WHY AM I FEELING SO DIZZY ALL OF A SUDDEN?

WHO KNEW IT'D BE SO EASY!
WHAT ARE YOU GUYS DOING HERE?
THE NURSE?!
WHISK
UM, WE...WE WERE JUST...
MY HEAD'S SPINNING!
I...UM...SUEE LEFT HER, UM... NOTEBOOK IN THE EXHIBIT ROOM BEFORE THEY CLOSED IT.
IS SHE ALL RIGHT? SHE'S SWEATING.
THEY...TOOK SUEE...TO THE NURSE...
I'M... FINE.
MAY I GO GET SUEE'S NOTEBOOK FOR HER? I WON'T BE LONG.
OH, YES, OF COURSE.

I HOPE YOU FIND IT.
SUEE, ARE YOU OK?
OF COURSE I AM...
ACTUALLY... SOMETHING'S... WRONG WITH ME...
RIGHT THERE.
THEY TOOK...SUEE... TO THE NURSE...
YEAH, RIGHT. I THINK SUEE'S A BIT SICK!
NO, I'M FINE.
IT FEELS LIKE MY WHOLE BODY'S FLOATING...
I'VE FELT THIS BEFORE...I CAN FEEL THE SHADOW TAKING OVER AGAIN...

I CAN SEE SOMETHING!
THAT'S THE POT WE SAW IN THE PICTURE!
SUEE, WHAT DO YOU THINK? IS THAT THE POT YOU SAW THAT DAY?
YES, THAT IS!
WHAT DID YOU JUST SAY?
YES...YES, IT IS...
HEY, YOUR FACE!
MY FACE? IT CAN'T BE!
HA! WHAT DID I TELL YOU?
NO! NOT NOW!

SUEE, YOUR SHADOW'S BACK!
WHY ARE YOU SO OBSESSED WITH THIS PLACE?!
WELL, IT DOESN'T MATTER NOW, BECAUSE I'LL MAKE YOU GET ME OUT OF HERE!
NO! I CAN'T GO BACK NOW! WE WERE ALMOST THERE!
SUEE, WHERE ARE YOU GOING!
WHEEL
YOU ARE SUEE'S SHADOW!
WHAT DID YOU THINK!
YOU KNOW THIS POT, DON'T YOU?

WH-WHAT POT? I DON'T KNOW WHAT YOU'RE TALKING ABOUT!
Y-YOU...DON'T?
SUEE...NURSE...THEY...TOOK... SUEE TO THE...NURSE...
HAEUN, WHY DO YOU KEEP SAYING THAT?
WAIT A SECOND...THEY TOOK SUEE TO THE NURSE ON HER FIRST DAY OF SCHOOL...
OH! I GOT IT NOW! THANKS, HAEUN!
YOU PASSED OUT IN THE EXHIBIT ROOM, ALMOST BROKE A VASE, AND ON TOP OF THAT, HURT YOUR HEAD...
SHE MUST'VE DROPPED IT ON THE FLOOR! SO THAT MEANS THERE MUST BE A...
I SAID I'D NEVER SEEN IT! PUT IT DOWN NOW!
EUREKA!

THERE'S A CRACK AT THE BOTTOM.
W-WHAT ABOUT IT?!
THIS MUST BE THE ONE SUEE ACCIDENTALLY DROPPED ON THE FLOOR THAT DAY! AND...
THIS IS THE POT FROM THE LEGEND!
W-WHAT ARE YOU IMPLYING?
THAT YOU ARE...
IF IT REALLY IS THE POT FROM THE LEGEND...
IT MEANS MY SHADOW IS...
THE POTTER'S DAUGHTER!

YES...THAT'S THE POT MY FATHER MADE A LONG TIME AGO. CURIOSITY GOT THE BETTER OF ME, AND I OPENED THE POT WHEN MY FATHER WASN'T LOOKING. THEN I WAS TRAPPED IN IT FOR WHAT SEEMED LIKE FOREVER.
I COULD VAGUELY HEAR PEOPLE TALKING, BUT I COULDN'T GET OUT OF THERE. YOU DON'T KNOW WHAT IT'S LIKE TO LIVE IN A POT.
THEN I LEARNED ONLY CHILDREN COULD OPEN IT.
AFTER I BECAME TRAPPED INSIDE THE POT, I GAINED THE ABILITY TO PEEK INTO CHILDREN'S SOULS—INTO ALL SORTS OF SECRETS WITHIN.
"MY GRADES ARE BAD."
"I'M THE ONLY ONE IN MY CLASS WHO DOESN'T HAVE AN IPHONE."
"KIDS BEAT ME UP."
"EVERYONE AT SCHOOL MAKES FUN OF ME."
"OK, MOM AND DAD GOT DIVORCED WHEN I WAS FIVE YEARS OLD."
"THESE GIRLS ARE NOT ON MY LEVEL."

IT WAS EASY TO CONVINCE THESE CHILDREN TO OPEN THE POT AND LET ME OUT. I ONLY HAD TO PRETEND TO BE NICE TO THEM.
ONCE THEY SET ME FREE, I TOOK THEIR SHADOWS, ONE BY ONE. THEIR SHADOWS WERE MORE VULNERABLE, AND THAT MADE IT MUCH EASIER FOR ME!
BUT WHY DID YOU HAVE TO TAKE THE SHADOWS AWAY?
BECAUSE THEN I'D HAVE A VOICE. I NEED A VOICE TO DRAW MORE CHILDREN TO THE POT.
I WAS ONLY BRIEFLY SET FREE FROM THE POT EVERY TIME A CHILD OPENED IT. BUT IT WAS DIFFERENT WHEN YOU DROPPED THAT POT, SUEE.
DO YOU KNOW HOW I FELT WHEN I SAW A RAY OF LIGHT COMING THROUGH THE CRACK IN THE BOTTOM?
SUEE, YOU SET ME FREE!
HMPH, WHOEVER THOUGHT THEY COULD COME IN HERE WITHOUT MY PERMISSION...
IT'S THE VICE PRINCIPAL!
...SHOULD EXPECT TO FIND THEMSELVES EXPELLED!

OH, DID I LEAVE THE DOOR OPEN?
NURSE?
YOU SEE, YOU SAID YOU WERE PLANNING TO USE THE SPACE FOR THE AFTER-SCHOOL PROGRAM, SO I WAS HOPING TO HELP BY CLEANING THINGS UP A BIT.
NO NEED. I WAS PLANNING ON LETTING MR. KANG'S COMPANY TAKE CARE OF ALL THE NETTLESOME CHORES.
LOVELY! SINCE YOU'RE HERE, WHY DON'T YOU COME BY MY OFFICE AND WE CAN REVIEW THE NEW LESSONS FOR THE AFTER-SCHOOL CLASS?
BONK
TEETER
TEETER
OH MY, HOW CLUMSY OF ME.
CRASH

WHAT WAS THAT ABOUT?
YES, THAT'S IT! I NEED TO TELL HYUNWOO!
SUEE? ARE YOU ALL RIGHT?
WHAT, NO, STOP!
RAM
WHAT ARE YOU DOING?!
SUEE...
SMASH
GAWK...
WHAT ARE YOU TRYING TO DO?

MY SHADOW SAID IT CAME OUT OF THE POT THROUGH THE CRACK. SO IF WE SMASH THE POT, HAEUN'S SHADOW MIGHT BE RELEASED!
ARE YOU...
TRYING TO SMASH THE POT?
PUT THAT THING DOWN!
YES, HYUNWOO!
ALL RIGHT, THEN! HERE WE GO!
STOP!
THUNK

IT WON'T BREAK. THIS IS DEFINITELY *NOT* AN ORDINARY POT.
WHY IS IT NOT WORKING? IT ALREADY HAS A CRACK IN THE BOTTOM.
WHEN I DROPPED IT, THE BOTTOM CRACKED OPEN AND RELEASED THE SHADOW.
MAYBE...
I'M THE ONLY ONE WHO CAN DESTROY IT!
SUEE, IT'S NO USE...
IT WON'T...WAIT, I THINK I KNOW WHAT YOU'RE THINKING...
YES, HYUNWOO, GIVE IT TO ME, NOW!

NOOOOO!!!
YOU CAN'T STOP ME NOW! I WILL FIND HAEUN'S SHADOW AND PUT IT BACK WHERE IT BELONGS!
STOP! WHAT IF IT REALLY WORKS?!
EVEN BETTER!
YOU WOULDN'T CARE IF I VANISHED? IF YOU LOST YOUR SHADOW FOREVER?
LOSE MY SHADOW... FOREVER? SO IF I DO THIS...I BECOME A ZERO?
YES, YOU FOOL! TOOK YOU LONG ENOUGH TO REALIZE THAT!
I DON'T WANT TO BE A ZERO!

DO YOU THINK ANYONE WOULD EVEN WANT TO TALK TO YOU IF YOU BECAME A ZERO? THEY'LL JUST WALK AWAY AND BE DONE WITH YOU!
IT'S THE SHADOW, ISN'T IT? SHE'S STOPPING YOU FROM BREAKING THE POT!
YOU CAN DO IT, SUEE! BEAT HER LIKE YOU'VE BEATEN HER BEFORE!
DID YOU HEAR THAT? HE WOULDN'T EVEN MIND IF YOU BECAME A ZERO!
ONCE I WAS TRAPPED IN THE POT, NO ONE CARED ABOUT ME ANYMORE!
BUT...
THINK ABOUT IT, I'M YOUR SHADOW! YOU CAN'T LIVE WITHOUT ME! BUT YOU DON'T NEED THEM!
BUT HAEUN IS MY FRIEND... MY FRIEND'S BECOME A ZERO. HOW CAN I JUST NOT CARE?

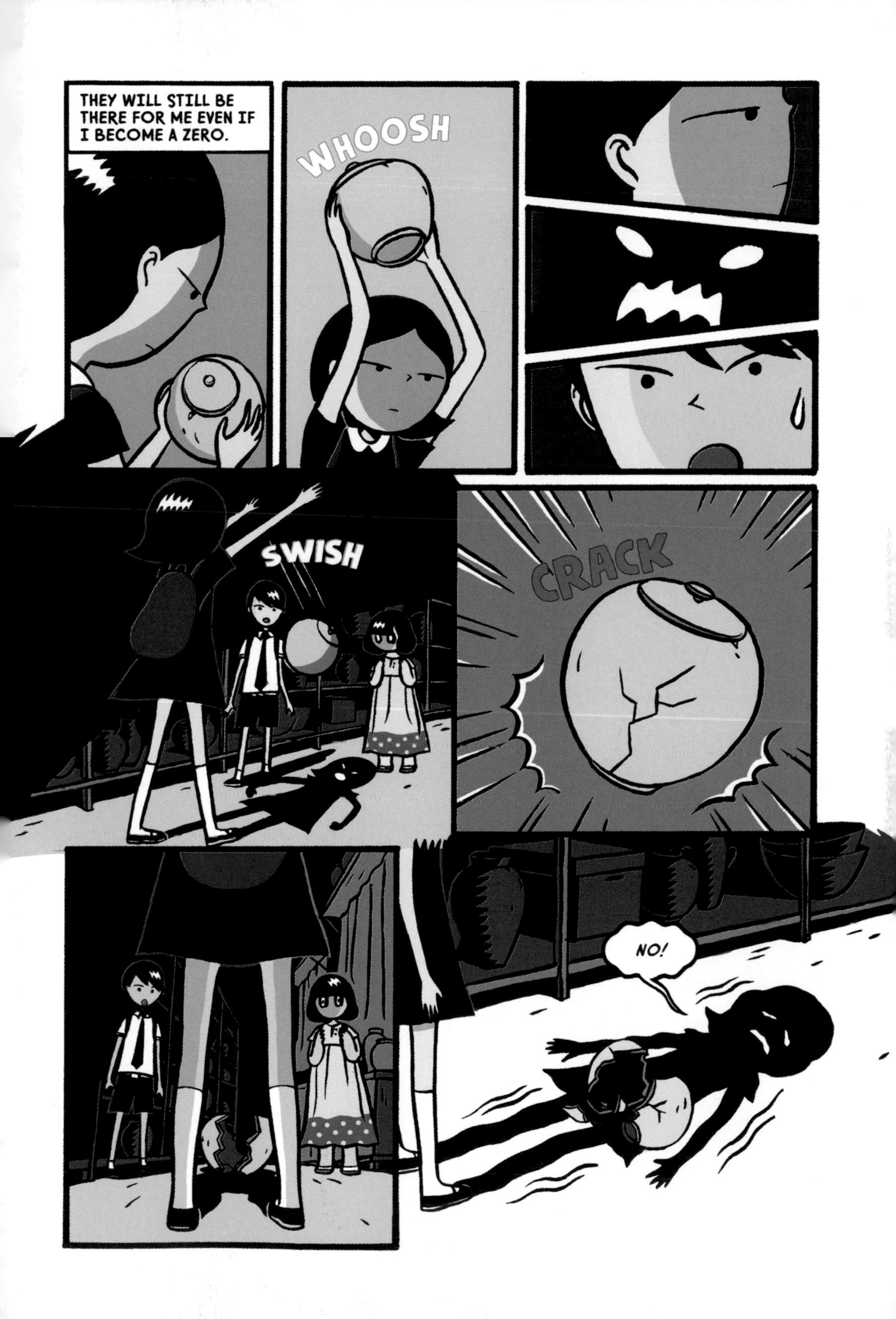
THEY WILL STILL BE THERE FOR ME EVEN IF I BECOME A ZERO.
WHOOSH
SWISH
CRACK
NO!

YOU CAN'T GET RID OF ME...
I'M YOUR SHADOW...
WHOOSH

WHERE AM I?
HAEUN, YOU'RE BACK!
HAEUN'S GOT HER SHADOW BACK!
IT'S ALL RIGHT, THEN.
BUT...WHAT'S GONNA HAPPEN TO ME?
SUEE...
ARE YOU OK?
AM I OK?
I DON'T KNOW.
BUT I'M SEEING THINGS. STRANGE THINGS...
I CAN SEE SHADOWS RETURNING TO THE OTHER KIDS.

AM I HAVING A NIGHTMARE?
BUT IT FEELS...PLEASANT.
ACTUALLY...IT FEELS KIND OF GREAT.
WE RETURNED THE SHADOWS TO THEIR OWNERS.
WE FOUND HAEUN'S SHADOW.

...SO THIS COMPANY BRIBED HIM IN EXCHANGE FOR ALL THAT CONSTRUCTION.
THE WHOLE AFTER-SCHOOL PLAN WAS FOR HIS OWN BENEFIT! HE WAS AFTER THE PRINCIPAL'S JOB!
OF COURSE HE WAS. HE WAS JUST TRYING TO GET A GOOD SCORE ON THE PERFORMANCE EVALUATION.
SERIOUSLY? AND THE PRINCIPAL HAD NO IDEA IT WAS HAPPENING RIGHT UNDER HER NOSE?
I'M SURE SHE KNEW BUT JUST DIDN'T CARE ENOUGH TO DO ANYTHING ABOUT IT. SHE'S RETIRING SOON.
MOM?! WHERE'S DAD? THE WHOLE SCHOOL'S FREAKING OUT OVER IT! THE POLICE ARE EVERYWHERE!
WHAT'S... GOING ON?
THEY'RE SAYING THE WHOLE AFTER-SCHOOL PLAN WAS THE VICE PRINCIPAL'S SCHEME TO TAKE THE PRINCIPAL'S JOB.
OH...
I WONDER HOW THE POLICE FOUND OUT ABOUT IT.
A SNITCH, OF COURSE.

WHAT'S A SNITCH?
A SNITCH IS AN INSIDE INFORMANT WHO EXPOSES ILLEGAL OR UNETHICAL ACTIVITIES OR ANY KIND OF WRONGDOING WITHIN AN ORGANIZATION.
YOU THINK ONE OF THE TEACHERS DID IT?
WHICH TEACHER?
THAT'S WHAT I WANT TO KNOW...WHO COULD IT BE?
OH, HELLO!
WHY IS HE IN SUCH A HURRY?
IT'S LIKE HE'S RUNNING AWAY...
HMM...I WONDER.

HAEUN GOT HER SHADOW BACK, AND THAT'S WHAT'S IMPORTANT!
HAEUN, MOVE JUST A LITTLE TO YOUR LEFT.
OK...
WE'RE BACK TOGETHER AGAIN AT OUR HIDEOUT.
OF COURSE, ZEROES NO LONGER EXIST IN SCHOOL.
BUT WE DECIDED TO KEEP OUR CLUB NAME. IT HAS A NICE RING TO IT, DON'T YOU THINK?
ZERO DETECTIVE CLUB
AS FOR THE SHADOW, I HAVEN'T SEEN HER SINCE THAT DAY IN THE EXHIBIT ROOM. I WONDER WHERE SHE'S GONE...
ZERO DETECTIVE CLUB
BUT SOMETIMES I GET THIS REAL UNCOMFORTABLE FEELING, LIKE THERE IS MORE TO COME...

LATER THAT NIGHT...

GINGER LY worked as a designer before earning her master's degree in filmmaking from the School of the Art Institute of Chicago. She lives in the suburbs of Seoul, South Korea.

MOLLY PARK lives in Seoul, South Korea, with two black cats and a mouse, and they all get along very well.

Suee and the Shadow is their debut graphic novel.

PUBLISHER'S NOTE: This is a work of fiction. Names, characters, places, and incidents are either the product of the author's imagination or used fictitiously, and any resemblance to actual persons, living or dead, business establishments, events, or locales is entirely coincidental.

Library of Congress Control Number 2017937935

Hardcover ISBN 978-1-4197-2563-0
Paperback ISBN 978-1-4197-2564-7

Illustrations by Molly Park
Cover and book design by B Hive, Inc. and Siobhán Gallagher
Translated by Keo Lee and Jane Lee

Printed in China
10 9 8 7 6 5

ABRAMS The Art of Books
195 Broadway, New York, NY 10007
abramsbooks.com